harmless scandals

A HARMLESS WORLD NOVEL

HARMLESS TROUBLE
BOOK THREE

MELISSA SCHROEDER

EDITED BY
NOEL VARNER

PHOTOGRAPHY BY
SCOTT CARPENTER

HARMLESS PUBLISHING

contents

also by melissa schroeder

THE HARMLESS WORLD

The Original Harmless Five

- A Little Harmless Sex
- A Little Harmless Pleasure
- A Little Harmless Obsession
- A Little Harmless Lie
- A Little Harmless Addiction

Rough 'n Ready

- Rough Submission
- Rough Fascination
- Rough Fantasy
- Rough Ride

Harmless Trouble

- Harmless Secrets
- Harmless Revenge
- Harmless Scandals

The Wulf Family

- Faith
- Taboo

- Trust

A Little Harmless Military Romance

- Infatuation
- Possession
- Surrender

Task Force Hawaii

- Seductive Reasoning
- Hostile Desires
- Constant Craving
- Tangled Passions
- Wicked Temptations
- Twisted Emotions

TFH Team Bravo

- Justified Secrets-coming soon

The Camos and Cupcakes World

Camos and Cupcakes

- Delicious
- Luscious
- Scrumptious

The Fillmore Siblings

- Hate to Love You
- Love to Hate You

Juniper Springs

- Wild Love
- Crazy Love
- Last Love
- Imperfect Love

THE SANTINI WORLD

The Santinis

- Leonardo
- Marco
- Gianni
- Vicente
- A Santini Christmas
- A Santini in Love
- Falling for a Santini
- One Night with a Santini
- A Santini Takes the Fall
- A Santini's Heart
- Loving a Santini

Semper Fi Marines

- Tease Me
- Tempt Me

- Touch Me

THE MELISSA SCHROEDER INSTALOVE COLLECTION

- Falling for my Best Friend
- Falling for my Baby Mama

Also Included

- Kiss my Tinsel
- Dad Bod Rockstar

Texas Temptations

- Conquering India
- Delilah's Downfall

Hawaiian Holidays

- Mele Kalikimaka, Baby
- Sex on the Beach
- Getting Lei'd

Once Upon an Accident

- The Accidental Countess
- Lessons in Seduction
- The Spy Who Loved Her

Telepathic Cravings

- Voices Carry
- Lost in Emotion
- Hard Habit to Break

Bounty Hunters, Inc

- For Love or Honor
- Sinner's Delight

Saints and Sinners

- Seducing the Saint
- Hunting Mila

Lonestar Wolf Pack

- Primal Instincts

Texas Heat

- Scorched

Spies, Lies, and Alibis

- The Boss

SINGLE TITLES

- A Calculated Seduction
- Chasing Luck
- Going for Eight
- Grace Under Pressure
- Operation Love
- Saving Thea
- Snowbound Seduction
- Sweet Patience
- The Last Detail
- The Seduction of Widow McEwan

Edited by Noel Varner

Cover Art by Scott Carpenter

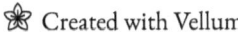 Created with Vellum

To Deana Potter whose joyous spirit, beautiful smile, and love for the romance genre never fail to amaze me.

hawaiian terms

Aloha - Hello, goodbye, love

Bra-Bro

Bruddah- brother, term of endearment

Haole-Newcomer to the islands

Hiwahiwa - precious

Howzit - How is it going?

Kamaʻāina-Local to the islands

Mahalo-Thank you

Malasadas- A Portuguese donut without a hole which started out as a tradition for Shrove (Fat) Tuesday. They are deep fried, dipped in sugar or cinnamon and sugar. In other words, it is a decadent treat every person must try when they go to Hawaii. If you do not try it, you fail. Do yourself a favor. Go to Leonard's and buy one. You are welcome.

Pupule - crazy

Slippahs - slippers, AKA sandals

T his time, Serenity thought, she would start out on the right foot with her neighbors.

She took the last loaf of banana macadamia nut bread out of the oven and set it on the rack to cool just as her phone rang. When she saw Nicola McCann's face on the screen, she answered it immediately.

"Good morning," she said.

"Good morning to you too. How's tricks?"

"Okay. Been working a lot. You?"

"Nothing much. We have some business trips coming up."

"Oh, you and the very delectable Jensen Wulf are going to be jet setting again? I thought that he had said he didn't want you going anywhere with him anymore."

One of their more recent trips had ended with Nicola and her boss in a massive fight. They worked well together, except when they had extra time on their hands. They tended to irritate each other in enclosed spaces.

"Jensen couldn't figure out how to get from point A to point B without me."

"I heard that," a male voice in the background said.

"He knows it. I know it. His mother knows it. So, did the new neighbors show up yet?"

At that moment, the rumble of a truck sounded on the path that led to the adjacent house. Set back away from Kam Highway, the only people who would be using that path would be she and her neighbors.

"Just happening right now. They've been busy all day." She peeked out the window to see the now familiar truck going past her house. Three men were sitting in the cab of the pickup, so that probably meant the woman Serenity had seen earlier was at that house.

"You haven't met them?"

"No, but they couldn't be any worse than my last neighbors."

"That's true. Who would have thought you bought a house next to a couple destined to act out *Who's Afraid of Virginia Wolf* every night?"

"Not me."

"Did they ever finalize the divorce?"

"I have no idea. Remember, I did not engage with them. Right now, I'm trying to forget they ever lived there, please. They were horrible."

A nasty divorce that had dragged out for two years. Neither husband nor wife would give up the house so they had lived there, together, making their lives and everyone who encountered them miserable.

"Okay. I must go now because Jensen lost his mind and scheduled breakfast with his mother; who, of course, wants me there. But, woman, please at least text me at some point if you won't call."

"You got it. I've been so busy with the book proposal, I've been losing track of time."

"That's good, but remember, I *will* call the HPD to check on you if I don't hear from you at least once a week."

With the power of Wulf Industries behind the threat, Serenity was pretty sure Nicola could make it happen.

"You got it."

After she clicked her phone off, she glanced at the loaves of mac bread. She'd been baking all day. It wasn't something she did all the time, but it was one of those simple joys she had discovered just a few years earlier. Baking was comfort.

It had been an odd idea for her to bake things for a neighbor. Serenity was proud of the fact that she was a tad antisocial. Avoiding people when she had spent her childhood trying to garner their attention, had been hard at first. Now it was almost second nature. Still, she wanted to be armed with information. If they were batshit crazy like her last neighbors, it was better to know now so she could avoid them.

After quickly wrapping a loaf from the earlier batch in plastic wrap, she donned her sunglasses and stepped out onto her lanai. She loved her little farmhouse, but it was nothing compared to her neighbor's house. They were both Kelly green, built around mid-century, and that was where the similarities ended. Serenity had never been inside the neighboring house. Most of the time, she avoided it if at all possible. The one time she made the mistake and walked within ten feet, the last owner explained she was divorcing her husband because he would fuck anything that moved.

Serenity still didn't know the woman's name.

She pushed that memory aside and took note of the beauty around her. Five years and she still couldn't believe she lived in Hawaii. A spur of the moment trip turned into so much more. The extra privacy in her house off the beaten path made her feel safe. The close proximity to a beach only locals usually went to made it even better. It was still kind of early in the day, so humidity hung in the air around her, holding the scent of plumeria that grew in front of her neighbors' house. When she walked up the steps to the front lanai, she heard the sound of paper being wadded up. She knocked on the screen door.

"Hold on," a woman's voice called out.

When the woman stepped into view, Serenity couldn't help but feel kind of frumpy.

The woman was average height, with light brown skin, and braids that swayed with each step she took. The bright blue sundress showed off amazing tattoos. Also, she was hugely pregnant.

"Hello," Serenity said. "I guess we're going to be neighbors."

The other woman blinked as if not understanding the words. The silence stretched as she continued to stare at her.

"I live just down the path," Serenity said, pointing behind her.

Her eyes widened. "Oh, oh! No, I don't live here." She was laughing when she opened the screen door. "Come on in. Sorry about that."

Serenity removed her slippahs and stepped into the house. She handed the woman the loaf.

"It's macadamia nut, just in case anyone is allergic."

"Thank you. My name is Jillian and I'm just a friend of the guys."

"Serenity."

"What?"

"My name is Serenity. Serenity Jones."

"Wow, that's a name."

"Thank you, I picked it out myself. So, it's just the guys moving in here?"

"Yes." Then after a moment of silence, Jillian laughed again. "Sorry. I can barely function in the last trimester. The hormones leave holes in my brain. Come on into the kitchen. Would you like something to drink?"

Serenity fought the urge to rub her hands on her board shorts. It was a nervous tick she'd had since her first days in acting. She hesitated, then reminded herself she needed to be friendly. This was why she made the bread and brought it over.

"Yes, just some water."

"Great, and I hope you don't mind drinking out of one of the guys' plastic stadium mugs. They have real things, but I am not doing *that* much unpacking for them."

"Not a problem at all."

"Great," she said smiling, then just stood there.

"Uh, water?"

She shook her head. "Okay, I'm now realizing that my husband might have a point and he isn't only being overly protective. He doesn't like leaving me alone." She motioned to the two bar stools. "Have a seat."

"So, the guys are the couple?"

She nodded. "Been together for a while. They insisted that they needed a bigger place though."

"Oh?"

She handed Serenity the water. "Yeah. No reason really. Knowing them, they just like things to be big. Men." She rolled her eyes. "So, do you work?"

Again, even after a decade as a normal person, Serenity had issues with giving people her background. She nodded. "Freelance photographer."

"Oh, do you do couples, or triples?"

"Of what?"

"People. I'm always on the lookout for a new person to bug for images."

"Uh."

Jillian rolled her eyes. "There I go again. They would be for my book covers. I'm an author."

"Oh. No. Sorry, I mostly do landscapes."

"Pity. Well, you probably have access to a lot of that here."

"It's what brought me here five years ago. I wanted to get some material, then I never left."

"I can understand that. I moved over here to hide from my family."

"That's a plus too."

"Just you then?" When Serenity didn't immediately reply, Jillian shook her head. "God, I sound like I'm pumping you for information. It's a writer's habit, but I'm usually more tactful than I have been today. I've just been stuck in here all day with no Wi-Fi. How is a chick supposed to survive without it?"

"I have no idea, especially since I need it to make a living."

She nodded. "Exactly. But, Conner said I had to come over here since our first demon seed is having a playdate and as you saw, my brain is mush."

Serenity smiled. "I would have gone crazy without Wi-Fi for a day. But yes, it is just me."

"Mick and Adam were happy to know there was someone living here and you weren't a renter."

"That definitely is a problem these days. I've heard some horror stories, especially on this side of the island since Obama made it so popular. It took them forever to redo the house, but I'll be happier with someone here."

"Oh?"

"I'm an independent woman with a huge imagination. Living off the beaten path is great, but it gets a little dark back here sometimes. And you never know when a drunk tourist will wander into the area."

"True." She settled in the chair next to Serenity's. "The

guys got the house at a great price. I heard it was because of the divorce."

"They had to redo the house from top to bottom after the war that was waged over here. More than once the police were called out."

"By you?"

She shook her head. "They would call the police on each other."

"Oh, god. That sounds like a nightmare."

"I avoided them as much as I could. Shame really. Two years ago, if it had been in good shape, they would have gotten top dollar for this place. But the yard and gardens need work and the housing market is leveling out a little bit. They had offers, but since the couple hated each other, they could never agree until they were forced to."

Jillian nodded. "The realtor said as much. I feel like we've met before."

"Excuse me?"

"Sorry. Dammit. Dying brain cells in a writer's mind is a recipe for disaster. You look familiar."

"No. I would definitely have remembered you."

"Oh, that's sweet. But..." she frowned, studying Serenity's face.

"Do you go to the Aloha Stadium Swap Meet?"

"Yes."

"I sell there sometimes. I'm usually not there to sell, but I've helped the vendor from time to time."

Once, and she felt guilty for lying. It wasn't like she hid the fact that she acted, but she didn't like talking about it at first. She didn't want anyone to think she was that girl anymore.

Before she would have to answer questions, she decided to head off. "I hate to drop off mac bread and run, but I have some work I have to do. Tell the guys if they need anything to just let me know."

"I will."

She walked up the path knowing it was a little rude to leave like that, but Serenity couldn't help it. She didn't mind people knowing she was a former child star, but she liked to keep it on the down low. She didn't need to deal with the press in her new life. It was always better to introduce her background to people slowly.

After she got back to her house, Serenity decided to worry about neighbors later. A girl had to eat, and to eat, she had to sell images.

two

M ick McGrath set down his last box just inside the door and sighed. Jillian held out a water bottle.

"Drink."

"Thanks." He opened the bottle and took a long drink.

"I think we're getting too old for this shit," he said.

"Make a hole," Adam said. Mick moved aside as he and Conner brought their last boxes in.

"Yeah, I know I'm too old for this," Conner said.

"Too old?" Jillian, Conner's wife asked as she walked in from the kitchen. She was six months pregnant and was in the waddle stage. Granted, they never let her know that was what they called it. "All I see standing in front of me are three fine male specimens."

"Well, this male specimen is tired and feeling his age," Conner said. The former FBI agent still wore his hair regulation short and didn't look a year over thirty.

She shook her head, her braids sliding over her bare shoulders.

"Please." She looked at the two of them. "And you two have food to eat anyway."

"Oh, you cooked?" Adam asked.

She laughed. "Yeah, no. It's hot today. I ran out and got you some Giovanni's shrimp, four servings because I know you two. Plus, your neighbor brought some food by."

Mick frowned. "I thought we'd never see her."

"Why's that?" Conner said as he opened a water bottle.

Mick shrugged. "Real estate agent said she's kind of quiet. Likes her privacy."

"Well, either way, she brought you some banana mac nut bread. And no, I didn't eat any. The thought of eating something sweet makes my stomach turn these days."

"What's she like?" Adam asked.

"She's rather tall, well over six feet."

"I like tall women," Mick said with a smile.

"I know you do. You hardly notice the hairy mole on her chin."

"Wait, what?"

She started laughing.

"She's rather petite, blond, and much too nice for the likes of you two."

"You are a sick woman playing with my emotions that way."

"I never claimed I wasn't. Now, Mr. Dillon, will you please take me home? I'm exhausted."

"Definitely."

"I know that both of you will want to get everything in order. But remember, you're not young hot studs anymore."

"So, what are we? Old hot studs?"

She shook her head. "Stop. Just don't overdo it. Both of you had that stomach bug last week." She rose up on her toes and gave each of them a kiss on the cheek.

"Behave and remember, dinner out tomorrow night. That way you don't have to worry about cooking tomorrow."

"Sounds good," Mick said.

"And if you don't come, I'll cry."

Adam rolled his eyes. "Yeah, sure."

"No. Please don't tempt her. Keep in mind, this is *pregnant* Jillian," Conner said.

"Oh, right," Mick said. Pregnancy did weird things to Jillian and her emotions. A woman who hardly ever cried and had an orderly mind, cried at the smallest things and couldn't remember what she was doing from one minute to the next. They followed them out to the lanai and waved as they drove off.

"She's going to text us three or four times tonight with things she already told us," Adam said.

Mick chuckled. "And which of us is going to tell her she already told us?"

"Not me. I'm not stupid."

They walked back into the house. There were boxes everywhere, packing paper littering the floor, and Mick knew they would have a massive pain in the ass to get it in order.

But a sense of relief and pride filled him. He took another swig of water.

"Hard to believe it's ours."

Adam chuckled. "Not really. We worked our asses off to buy it."

It had been three years they had been saving for the house. They wanted something like this that gave them privacy but near the beach. It was hard to find that on Oahu today, without spending several million dollars.

Mick turned to step in front of him. "And it's all ours," he said cupping Adam's face in his hands. He leaned in, pressed his mouth against Adam's. And just like the first time they kissed, the rush of excitement flowed through him, along with the familiarity of old lovers. They were both sweaty, tired, and he could feel Adam's cock pressed against his. Fuck.

"Time to christen the house, I think." Even he heard the arousal in his voice, the deepening of his tone.

Adam smiled. It was that same fucking smile that had drawn Mick in from the start. He'd always had a crush on his friend, but after years of keeping his distance, he had taken a chance. He thanked God every day since.

Adam kissed him, pressing his mouth against Mick's. He traced the seam of Mick's lips with is tongue, and he didn't hesitate. Mick opened his mouth and Adam stole inside. Before Mick was satisfied, Adam was moving away, kissing a path down his neck.

"Hmm, hot, sweaty man," he growled against Mick's flesh. He nipped at the pulse point then drew the flat of his tongue across it. Mick shivered. Adam chuckled, his breath fanning out over Mick's sensitive skin.

Need surged. Mick didn't even care that Adam was in control, or that he felt the need to take charge tonight. He wanted to be taken, to lose himself in everything Adam could make him feel.

Adam slipped his fingers under the hem of Mick's shirt. Slowly, he pulled the fabric up, letting his fingers skim over Mick's abs.

He groaned.

"What's the matter, babe?" Adam asked as he tugged the shirt over Mick's head, tossing it behind him. He immediately attacked Mick's neck again. Of course he did. He knew what got Mick hot, and his neck was definitely one place.

Damn.

"I gotta have you now," Mick growled.

"The bed isn't put together," Adam said, humor lacing his voice.

"We don't need a bed."

"Of course not." Adam took a step back, then dropped to his knees in front of Mick.

Adam unzipped Mick's shorts. He didn't hesitate. Adam wrapped his hand around Mick's cock. Mick jerked as Adam tightened his fingers slightly, then started to stroke him. Mick closed his eyes, and leaned against the counter.

"Fuck, yeah," he said, moving in rhythm with Adam's hand.

"Watch me," Adam demanded.

It took all of Mick's control to open his eyes and look

down his body. Adam waited until he made eye contact, then, he took Mick's cock into his mouth. He kept his gaze locked with Mick's as he swirled his tongue over the head of his dick, then closed his eyes and hummed as he took it into his mouth again. The vibrations filtered through his whole body. He was close, so fucking close. He knew that with one, maybe two more thrusts, he would come. Adam knew him too well. He pulled away and Mick growled.

He laughed and rose, slipping his hands up Mick's body as he did. Adam cupped his face then gave him a long, wet kiss. Even so, it was over before Mick was ready.

Adam stepped back, tugged out of his shirt and shorts as Mick stepped out of his shorts. Mick eyed Adam's cock, the head of it wet with precum, but Adam didn't give him the chance to do or say anything. He spun Mick around, bending him over the counter. Mick could tell he was no longer in complete control. His movements held a sense of urgency that fueled Mick's own arousal. Knowing he could get to Adam this way was one of the most erotic things in life.

Adam thrust into him hard and they both groaned in appreciation.

"Yes," Adam muttered as he began to move in and out of Mick's ass. He leaned down and kissed his neck as he continued to thrust. Their groans mingled with the sound of their flesh slapping. Adam slipped his hand down to Mick's cock and started to stroke him. His fingers teased him, pushing him closer to his orgasm. He was so close, so ready to come, but he wanted to wait. He wanted to do it with Mick.

It didn't take his lover long to catch up.

"Come with me, babe," Adam said. Raw need filled his voice as he begged him to come. He could no longer hold back. Adam thrust into him one last time.

Together they groaned, Mick shuttered as his release took over his body, his mind. They collapsed together against the counter, their heavy breathing the only sound.

"That was one hell of a christening," Adam said with a chuckle as his kissed Mick's neck.

"It was, but you're killing me here. Move."

"You expect me to move after that?" Adam asked, but he did as Mick asked. When he turned around, Mick took Adam's face into his hands, just as Mick had done to him earlier.

"I love you," he said. Then he kissed him, keeping his gaze locked with Adam's. This wasn't erotic, but more sweet. He wanted Adam to always know that he was his, that nothing would ever come between them. Even after all their years together, he knew that Adam worried.

He pulled back and rested his forehead against Adam's.

"I love you, too," Adam said.

"How about I find a bottle of that Pino Gris and we heat up that shrimp for dinner?"

Adam smiled. "I'll find the wine, you do the shrimp."

"Maybe we should put some clothes on."

Adam glanced around and Mick laughed when he saw

his expression. He wasn't a prude, but he knew Adam would get irritated that the window had been left wide open.

"Don't worry. No one's around."

"But our neighbor," Adam muttered as he stepped into his shorts and pulled them up.

He grabbed Adam's hand. "Hey, no one saw. We just need to get some blinds just in case from now on."

He smiled. "Yeah."

Mick squeezed his hand, then released it. "Now that we've christened the house with sex, it's time for our first meal."

SERENITY PUT HER CAMERA DOWN WITH SHAKING hands. *Damn.* She hadn't intended on being a peeping Tom. She had seen the rainbow and it was particularly bright. She'd finished snapping a shot and was swinging around to her own front yard when she saw them.

Damn. Well, hell, she had already thought that. She needed another word, but her mind was just a bit blank. The raw sexuality she had just watched left her without the ability to think. Her pulse thundered in her throat as she tried to get her breathing under control. Hell, her nipples were hard and she was damned sure her panties were wet.

Growing up in Hollywood, she had seen a lot of things. So much so, she rarely was shocked or aroused by public displays of affection or nudity. Or really, anything. Of course, that was different from what she had just witnessed. This was love.

She had witnessed the kiss. Affection and lust, need, desire...it was all there. It had intrigued her, made her heart do that little skip it always did. It was possibly one of the sexiest kisses she had ever seen. She knew she should have looked away, but then, when the situation had turned carnal, she couldn't seem to turn away.

Of course, she was turned on by two guys having sex. Figures. Hollywood had warped her. She was a voyeuristic freak. It didn't trouble her that it had been two men. Even through her lens, she could see just how sexy they were, and if she had met them before this incident, she would have found them sexy. Two men who looked like them having sex would turn on anyone with a brain. No, what bothered her was that she was more aroused watching them than she had been the last time she had sex.

She could almost hear them shout as they came. She closed her eyes and counted backwards from ten. Then she did it again. It took her two more times to get her libido under control.

After draining her glass of water, she headed off to the bathroom. An ice-cold shower was definitely in order.

three

The next morning, Serenity was on her second cup of coffee and steaming through work by eight. Like most mornings, she was up with the sun, but she was a little tired. The visions of her neighbors kept coming to her in dreams. And worse, she could probably pass them on the street and never know it was them. She hadn't even tried to look at their faces yesterday. That was how much of a perv she was. She could have, if she'd tried, but she hadn't. Her mother was right, she was probably going to hell.

The morning breeze brought the sound of male voices through her window. At first it was just the rumble of masculine voices, but the closer they got, she picked up on the conversation.

"I say it's kind of like being a stalker," a man said.

"I say it isn't because we haven't met her. Besides, it's nice to thank someone for food, especially if you want any more of that bread ever again."

"Good point. Definitely want more of that delicious bread."

"Even if she had a hairy mole on her chin."

What the hell did that mean?

A few seconds later, someone knocked on her door. With reluctance, she walked to the door. Normally, it was just dealing with people when she wanted to work. Today, it was something different. She had watched them have sex and now she would have to pretend all was normal. They didn't know what she had seen but she would know. She had never been *that* good of an actress.

When she approached the door, she felt her body get hot again. She could just imagine the sounds they made during sex. And why was she thinking about that right now? She should be imagining snow. And icebergs.

She drew in a deep breath and then released it slowly before she opened the door.

All thoughts of the coming ice age dissolved at the sight of all the male beauty in front of her.

One had dark blond hair and possessed the most amazing blue eyes. He was wearing a faded t-shirt that seemed to be a size too small. Good god he had muscles. But then, so did the other one. He was just a little taller, had brown hair and the most incredible green eyes. Both were tanned, and smiling.

She almost melted into a big puddle right there at their feet.

"Hey," the brown haired one said. "We're your neighbors that just moved in."

Oh, no. His smiled widened and it made him adorable.

"You're my only neighbors," she said with a chuckle. And because she knew she was being rude, she opened the screen door and stepped out.

His smile transformed into a grin. Oh damn. "My name is Mick and this is Adam."

She smiled. "My name is Serenity, but I'm sure Jillian told you."

"No, she didn't. Her brain is kind of mushy," Mick said.

"She did mention that."

"We just wanted to thank you for the bread," Adam said. "It really hit the spot."

"You ate it all already?"

"We had the coffeemaker unpacked but not much else. We had it for breakfast," Mick said.

"And you want some more? I mean, that *is* what you said."

She glanced at Adam whose mouth twitched. He leaned closer to Mick. "You have a big mouth."

"I also don't think of it as stalking."

There was a moment of silence, then they both started laughing.

"Damn, maybe Jillian was right. We *are* loud," Mick said.

"And, I do have an extra loaf if you want it."

"Yes," they both said at the same time. God, they were so cute.

"Let me get it for you."

She stepped into her house and rushed over to the free-standing kitchen island, grabbed the loaf and then returned to the guys. They hadn't moved an inch.

"We will take this on one condition," Mick said.

"And that would be?"

"Come to dinner with us tonight."

She blinked, trying to discern his tone. It was almost like he had asked her out for a date with the two of them.

"Good God, Mick. You sound like a creeper," Adam said, shaking his head. "What he means is that we are going out to eat with Jillian and her husband Conner tonight. We would love to have you join us."

"Oh. Hmm."

Adam bumped Mick's shoulder with his own. "See, you scared her off."

"I did not. What an idiotic thing to say."

"You two do know I am standing here, right?"

They turned to face her.

"Sorry," Mick said.

She waved it away. "First, I hesitated because I needed to think about my schedule. But I do believe I am free tonight."

"Great."

"What time?"

"What?" Mick said.

Adam rolled his eyes. "Seven tonight at Haleiwa Beach House. We'd offer a ride, but we have to run some errands beforehand."

"No worries. I've been wanting to try that place since they opened."

"Good," Mick said.

"Great," Adam said.

Then they stood there staring at her. She had to fight the urge to laugh.

"Did you need anything else?"

They both had the most adorable blushes.

"No. We'll see you tonight," Adam said, as he hit Mick. It took him another couple of seconds to respond. He dipped his head.

"Thanks again for the bread."

They turned and walked back to their house. She watched them, realizing that she'd actually made it through the conversation without telling them she had seen them naked. And — having hot sex. Really, really hot sex.

She rolled her eyes and went back into her house. Work would keep her busy and get her mind off her neighbors. She would have to deal with it at dinner tonight though, but she had time to mentally prepare herself not to be a perv. Maybe.

"So, you both went over to her house and asked her out?" Jillian said, the laughter easy to hear in her voice.

Adam nodded. "Mick just had to go over there this morning."

Mick glanced at his lover, then back to Jillian. "You *are* supposed to thank people who give you food, right? And you wanted to go over there as much as I did."

He ignored the comment. It was true that he had wanted

to go over there, but he hadn't expected to make a fool of himself. Mick had also, but he didn't give a damn.

"Either way, she was up and we invited her here tonight. You don't mind, do you?"

She shook her head, her braids spilling over her shoulders. She was the picture of maternal beauty, wearing a yellow sundress and a head scarf to match. "No. In fact, I'm glad to have another woman at the table to even the playing field."

"There's three of us," Mick pointed out.

She snorted. "It takes at least one and one-half of a man's brain to outsmart a woman."

Adam looked at Conner. "Do you let her talk to you like this all the time?"

"No comment."

Jillian laughed and opened her mouth to say something, but something caught her attention just over Adam's shoulder. He turned to see what snagged her attention, and promptly lost all his rational thought.

Serenity was walking through the restaurant. Jillian had been right, she called her small in stature, but her presence did not go unnoticed. She strode through the tables, a smile on her face.

The dress she wore was a simple with Hawaiian white print against a red background. It didn't even hug her curves and barely showed a hint of cleavage, but it was the sexiest thing he'd seen lately.

By the time she made it to the table, he was already

standing and pulling out the chair between Mick and him. That's when he noticed that Mick was standing also.

"Hey," she said, a bit breathless. "Sorry I'm late."

They said nothing for a long moment.

"No worries," Jillian said, her voice filled with amusement. "Why don't you have a seat?"

"Thanks." When she sat down, both he and Mick sat down.

"This is my husband Conner. Conner, this is Serenity Jones."

She smiled and Adam wasn't too sure that he didn't sigh out loud. She had the best damned smile.

"It's nice to meet you."

The waitress appeared and took her drink order.

"How is the unpacking going?" she asked.

"We have the kitchen done," Adam said.

"Most important thing," Serenity said.

"You cook a lot?" Jillian asked.

"Not really. Living alone makes it annoying, but having the kitchen up and running is more about food. I love food."

Jillian rubbed her tummy. "I have to agree with you."

"Have we met before?" Conner asked

She shook her head. "I don't think so. What do you do for a living?"

"Former FBI. Now I deal with security."

She chuckled. "Then not that way. At least I don't think I've ever been under investigation."

Conner smiled. "You just look very familiar."

"Hmm," was her only response before the waitress stepped up to take their food orders.

"I take it you're not a local," Mick said.

She shook her head. "Although, I've lived here the longest of my adult life. I've been here five years."

"How long have you been a photographer?" Jillian asked.

"You're a photographer?" Mick asked.

"I started when I was sixteen. I was just lucky enough that I can make a living off it. The rise of online royalty free sites allows me to live where I want, and there is always a demand for Hawaiian scenery."

"You can work from home then?"

She nodded. "I know what Conner and Jillian do, but what do you two do?"

She turned her head and made eye contact with Adam. He had the answer on the tip of his tongue, but his ability to speak died the moment her whiskey-colored eyes connected with his. She turned and smiled at him. Her eyes lit up and she had two of the most adorable dimples. Oh, damn, he was fucked.

"Um."

"Yes?" she asked smiling.

"We work security," Mick said, saving him.

She turned away and Adam could finally let loose of the breath that had been caught in his throat. He didn't dare glance over in Jillian's direction. She'd detect his feelings and then she would meddle. Jillian rarely meddled but when she was pregnant, she didn't seem to be able to help herself.

He pushed those thoughts aside as a few strands of her honey blonde hair had escaped the bun she had on the top of her head. He had to fight the urge to reach over and touch.

"Security?"

"We handle a few things here and there, work on contract."

"If I could get them signed on as permanent employees, I would be thrilled," Conner said.

"You'd expect us to come into work every day. You know how that would never work for us," Mick said.

"If you wanted to, you could find a way."

"Then we would get in a fight, quit, and then Jillian would have to leave you. Do you want that?" Mick asked.

Conner just smiled and shook his head. "You know that's bullshit."

Mick waved that comment away as the waitress returned with the appetizers they ordered earlier.

"I hope you don't mind, but mama needed to eat, so I got us some apps," Jillian said.

"No worries. As I said, food is very important to me," she said, taking a plate and filling it with tuna tartar. "I have a very serious relationship with it."

"And that comes from?" Adam asked.

She smiled as she placed her napkin on her lap. "I had to keep what photographers claimed was "fit" when I was a teen. Imagine being a teen and being told you couldn't have pizza. It was horrible."

From her aggrieved tone, he knew she was joking, but there was a hint of something else beneath it. She joked, but there was also pain of some sort.

"Photographers?" Mick asked. "Were you a fashion model?"

She laughed out loud at that. So loud, in fact, it drew attention from some nearby diners.

"Uh, no. Too short for that. But I did some hair shots, things like that."

"Hair shots?"

"Yeah, they use body parts of other people for ads. Like, I had a friend who was just a hand model. Her hands were in all kinds of ads."

"Oh, I've heard of that, but I wasn't sure if it was true."

She nodded as she popped some tuna into her mouth. "My eyes were used too, so maybe that's it," she said to Conner. "I was in a lot of ads there for a while, but my entire face wasn't."

"Could be," he said, but Adam knew from his tone Conner didn't think it was that.

Adam didn't think it was, but he knew just from the short discussion this morning and now, that Serenity prized her privacy. Adam could understand. She had apparently made a living as a kid being shoved in front of the camera. Someone like that would either love it or hate it. She had apparently hated it. So, for now, he would happily give her the privacy she wanted and wouldn't question her.

Adam leaned back in his chair and watched as she and Jillian discussed something about the new rail system.

Serenity was animated in the discussion, and he couldn't help but smile at a few of her sarcastic comments.

Mick caught his eye. There was no doubt he was thinking the same thing. The woman was a delight. Sexy, funny, and smart. Three things that they always liked in their women. Mick would start pushing soon, but Adam wanted to take his time.

Presents were always more interesting when you unwrapped them slowly.

four

Serenity rolled over the next morning and groaned. The first rays of soft light were already peeking into her bedroom. She had spent the night without sleep. *Again*. She sat up and let out another groan. Why had she been having so many insane dreams? She wasn't a prude, but she had never thought that seeing two men having sex would cause her so many problems.

She stared at her ceiling and thought back to the night before. Adam and Mick had been very welcoming. She had pretty much spent most of her time on Oahu sort of separate from other people. She wasn't a hermit or a shut in. She found it easier if she limited her time with other people though. Last night had her second guessing what she had seen.

Having spent almost her entire childhood in Hollywood, Serenity had good gaydar. Many people would look at men like Mick and Adam and assume they were just friends. Even with them living together, their build and their masculinity would give people false impressions of their sexuality. Serenity knew better. Masculinity had nothing to do with sexual preference, as her dance teacher had been one of the most effeminate men she had ever met, and he was *definitely* heterosexual.

Knowing she would get no sleep, and since she was already sweaty, she decided to go for a run on the beach. It was better she worked off this energy than sat here thinking about her insanely sexy neighbors. If she got it done early enough, she would be ready when her friend Dai came by to discuss business.

MICK WAS TAKING HIS FIRST SIP OF COFFEE THAT morning, sitting on their back lanai, when he saw Serenity. She came running up the path that led down to the beach. She was dressed for running and her body glistened with her exertion.

"Hey," he called out. She stopped and headed in his direction. He tried not to get too excited. She was probably just being friendly.

"Hey, yourself," she said with a smile, looking up at him.

Damn.

"Are you always an early riser?"

She nodded. "I hate it. I would love to be able to roll around in bed. And you?"

"My military roots. Dad was military and I followed in

his footsteps. But I agree, rolling around in bed is much more interesting."

She didn't respond to that. Instead, she looked off into the distance. Worried he had made her uncomfortable, he opened his mouth to rectify it, but Adam interrupted him.

"I wake up all alone and find you out here flirting with our neighbor."

She turned to face them both, a smile curving her lips. Mick wished he could see her eyes, but they were hidden behind her mirrored sunglasses.

"Not much flirting. He didn't even offer me anything to drink."

Adam looked at Mick. "I thought I trained you better."

He shrugged and looked over at Serenity. "He tries, as did my mother."

"You're telling me that you are untrainable?"

"Not in the important things."

She chuckled. "I need to go take a shower so you'll have another chance to impress me with your hospitality manners another time."

She waved as she hurried off.

"Tsk, tsk, tsk," Adam said.

"What?" Mick asked as he watched Serenity as she disappeared around the corner of their house.

"I think someone has a crush." Adam leaned closer. "Someone might just be thinking of some naughty things to do with Serenity."

Mick turned his head and kissed him on the cheek.

"I guess I should point out that you have one too. I saw the way you reacted to her last night."

Adam stepped back as he smiled. Mick turned around to face him.

"What are you talking about?"

He snorted. "Please, you looked like you wanted to take one huge bite out of her at dinner."

A flush darkened Adam's face.

Mick laughed, set his coffee down on the table, then pulled him closer for a hug. "You are so predictable, but this time I definitely agree."

"I don't think it's a good idea though."

"Why not?"

Adam pulled away, then walked into the kitchen. "I need coffee if we're going to talk about this."

Shaking his head, Mick grabbed his coffee and followed him. Adam liked playing with a third, which was always a woman for the two of them.

Adam was already sipping his coffee when Mick stepped into the kitchen.

"You think it's a good idea to fool around with our neighbor? Really?"

Mick shrugged. "I didn't say it was a good idea, but it is a delicious idea."

Adam rolled his eyes. "And it could make everything awkward. Can you imagine if we proposition her and she turns us down?"

"Well—"

"Worse, what if she says yes and it goes badly, or even if it goes well, but she doesn't want to continue? Then we have ruined our chances at having a normal relationship with our one and only neighbor."

"All good points."

Adam groaned. "I hate that fucking tone."

Mick smiled. "What tone?"

"The one that tells me you won't pay any fucking attention to me at all."

"I understand your misgivings, and it isn't like I'm going to march over there today and ask her about joining in with a threesome."

Adam's frown eased. "I know that. I just don't want you to get your hopes up."

Mick sighed, knowing that Adam wasn't being an ass on purpose. It was a knee jerk reaction and Mick understood why. He wished he could make it easier for Adam to accept that someone else might love him the way that Mick did. Raised by an abusive mother, then landing in the foster system when she abandoned him, Adam was very wary of strangers. Of anyone, really. It took Mick years to get him to believe he loved him.

"We've talked about a third for the past few years."

"Yeah and you thought it was Jillian to begin with."

"Well, she is into the lifestyle."

"But not for us."

"And have I talked about it again?"

"Yes."

"Not seriously. And I'm not saying she's the one, but I like her, and you do too. It is hard to find a woman who both of us like."

"That's true."

"Listen, I'm not saying she's going to be into it, but it is something we should think about."

"I don't know why this is so important to you."

"To us. Don't tell me when we play at Rough 'n Ready it doesn't get you hotter than when we're alone. Neither of us enjoy being the sub, but we like to dominate. Having a woman allows that."

Adam sighed. "I know, but I also think that it can't be just any woman. It needs to be the right woman."

"Okay. We need to get to know her better."

Adam nodded, but he still didn't look happy about it.

"Hey," Mick said, pulling him closer, he pressed his mouth against Adam's. He slipped his tongue inside for a taste, just a taste. He regretfully pulled back because they didn't have time to play. "One day at a time."

He nodded. "So, you handle the bedroom? I'll do the living room."

"Sounds good."

He'd throw himself into getting the house in order, then he could start working on a plan to get to know Serenity better.

five

F our hours later, Adam sat on one of the breakfast bar stools. Every muscle in his body was aching, but the house was starting to come together. "I think we made a big dent in the house today," Adam said as he took a long swig of beer.

"Yeah," Mick said looking out the front window.

"Stop doing that."

"What?"

"You look like a creeper."

He shook his head, but didn't move his gaze away from the direction of Serenity's house.

"What?"

"There's a dude over there."

"And?"

"Well, just, I didn't think she was involved with anyone."

"She never said that," Adam said. "You assumed because you wanted her so badly."

"Still, she went out with us."

"She didn't go out with us. She had dinner with a group."

Wanting a look at the guy because Adam couldn't help himself, he frowned when he saw the truck.

"There's no guy."

"I saw the back of him when he went into her house."

"Don't get like this. She can have friends. Hell, she can have lovers."

Mick tossed him an angry look.

"Tell me you don't want her."

"For fuck's sake, Mick, we just met her. She had a whole life before us. And again, you're creeping me out, so I am sure you will creep her out by this behavior."

Mick grunted, and returned his gaze back to the house.

This was a bad sign. Mick was already starting to obsess, and that could be a problem. He wasn't a weirdo, but he tended to latch onto ideas. Once he did, he could never let them go. It usually ended with him being horribly disappointed and broody. And then Adam would have to kick his ass.

"Mick." No response. "Vincent."

He made a face, but finally turned his attention away from Serenity's house. That was half the battle won.

"I know you're attracted. I am too. But she's our neighbor and she seems like a sweet woman. Let's take it one day at a time. If she's involved with someone, it isn't any of our business."

"But... Shit. You're right."

Adam watched Mick as he walked over to the kitchen table and sat down. He followed him and continued to study him.

"What's up? There's something else bothering you."

He shrugged and tore at his beer label. "Nothing really."

"Mick, you don't go all depressed on me unless there's something nagging at you."

He sighed. "We're good, if that's what you're worried about."

He wasn't really, but he knew this would just fester if he let it go. Setting his beer on the counter, he stepped in front of Mick, and settled his arms over his shoulders.

"I know that, but there's something else. Something that's bugging you."

"I don't know, really. We got the house, now what?"

He should have known. Mick was a happy person. Constantly in a good mood, even at six in the morning. But, he leaned toward being goal oriented. His parents had raised him that way. It made him a kick ass security expert, but sometimes, it made it hard to live with him. He just didn't always seem to understand goals are good, but they don't always come to fruition.

"Are we missing anything in our lives? Do we need anything else?"

He sighed. "Not sure. I just..."

Now he was getting worried as he studied Mick's bent head.

"Spit it out."

"It's stupid because I have always been okay with us. I love you and don't want to ever lose you."

"But?"

"I want children."

He blinked. "What?"

"I want children, and I want a woman in our lives. Like permanently."

"Huh."

Mick glanced up at him. "See, that's why I never said anything. I didn't want you to think that I found anything lacking between us."

"But, apparently, you do."

He tried to drop his hands, but Mick grabbed one and brought it up to his mouth. He pressed his lips against the inside of his wrist.

"I want you in my life forever, but I think we both need a woman here. We're bisexual, not homosexual. It is unconventional to even think about it, but I think our lives would be better with a woman."

"In what way?"

Mick threaded his fingers through Adam's. "Maybe we need someone to complete us."

"That's...corny."

He smiled and leaned up to brush his mouth against Adams. That little taste had his heart racing.

"Yes, but did we buy this big house just so Mom and Dad have a place to stay? I don't think so. We were both thinking of the future. We can adopt, but I know both of us would like to try to have children. We need a woman in our lives for that."

"We could use a surrogate."

Even before he finished the sentence, Mick was shaking his head.

"It isn't just that. You know what I'm talking about, right? Together we have an edge. Masculine, wonderful," he said as he released Adam's hand and cupped his face with one hand. He brushed his thumb over his mouth. "But, with a woman, we could soften that edge. Maybe, I'm going senile in my old age, but I like us when there's a woman with us in bed. I'd really like to see what it's like when she's in our life."

"First, you aren't old. And I get what you're saying." And he did, even though he wasn't completely sold on it. "It doesn't mean it has to be Serenity."

"No. But, she's..." he sighed.

"Yeah. She is."

His gaze moved past Adam to Serenity's house. "There she is."

Mick popped up off the barstool and headed for the door.

It was a good thing he loved Mick, or he might just have to kill him.

"THOSE ARE GOING TO SELL, SERENITY," DAI SAID as she followed him out the door.

"Are you sure?"

He smiled at her. He was about ten years older, had the kindest heart, and she counted him as one of her few friends in Hawaii. That's why she turned him down when he asked her out a couple years ago. He hadn't let that get in the way of their working relationship.

"You always ask me that. They will sell. How's the book coming?" He stepped into his slippahs.

"Okay. Slow."

"You'll get it done and everyone will love it."

"I think I should call you daily so I can have you say nice things to me."

He chuckled. "I gave you that choice, Hiwahiwa. You turned me down. Now I am happily married."

"To Sherry, who is your soul mate, so I think I deserve a call every day just for that."

He chuckled and gave her a hug. "I'll get those printed up in the next couple of weeks."

"Sounds good," she said as she released him.

"Hey," Mick said.

She blinked. "Oh, hey, Mick. Howzit?"

"Going well. We have the bedroom and living room set up."

Adam came up behind him, a look of apology on his face. She had no idea what that was about.

"Dai, this is Mick and Adam. They bought the *War of the Roses* house."

"Ah, well it's good to know there is finally someone out here by you."

"I can take care of myself."

"I know you can, but Sherry worries."

She rolled her eyes as he kissed her cheek. He gave her a wink the other men couldn't see. "I'll let you know when I get those printed up and they are for sale."

"Thanks," she said.

"Nice to meet you two."

Then he climbed into his pickup.

"Was there something you needed?"

"No," Mick said. Adam rolled his eyes.

"Sorry. Mick just wanted to stretch his legs. He goes a little nuts being stuck inside all day."

"Okay." She wanted to invite them in. She wanted to touch them. And there it was. That bit of her that was going to hell.

"Well, I don't want to be rude, but I'm going out for some shoots this afternoon."

"No worries," Mick said smiling at her. "We still have a ton of crap to do. Just wanted to say hey."

As she watched them walk back to their house, she shook her head. They were sexy and cute. Sweet even. But they were not for her. They were together and that was all that mattered. She would have to remember that and just fantasize about them when she was alone.

Six

A week later, Serenity was finally back on track. She'd spent the day out on the North Shore shooting the massive waves thanks to the storm hitting. When a storm this big hit, waves could cover Kam Highway and she'd have to take the long way around home.

She grabbed her raincoat and waterproof camera. She wanted to get some pics of the storm before it moved into her area.

She hurried down the path to the beach, the rain pelting against her skin so hard it hurt. The wind danced through the trees and left her unable to hear anything but that.

"I have to be insane. Like straight up legit insane."

And, she was talking to herself again. A sure sign of insanity.

She ignored everything and let the electricity from the storm feed into her creativity. She reached the beach and found a few folks gathered to watch the approaching storm.

Hawaii rarely got storms this big without a name attached to them.

She found a good space without anyone near her and started to snap a few pics. The dark, threatening clouds against the breaking waves made a dramatic backdrop, and she knew they would be popular with her followers. In fact, she might get a few of these printed up for Dai. They would sell well at his shop, but also at the Aloha Swap Meet. Or, she could keep them to include in her book she was working on.

"Hey," a male voice shouted over at her.

She jumped, then noticed it was Mick. It had been days since she'd talked to either of her neighbors. She had seen them a lot, but from her window, or a wave to them on their lanai.

"Hey, yourself."

"What the hell are you doing out here?"

"Pics," she said holding up her camera.

"You're crazy."

She laughed. "I was just thinking the same thing."

The rain started to pour harder and the wind changed directions.

"I think you should get inside."

She nodded and started back to the path that lead to their houses. He followed her, then when the path widened stepped up beside her.

With the trees taking some of the rain off them, Serenity looked at him. Okay, he was still ridiculously beautiful. Even with his dark hair plastered against this head, he looked good enough to eat. He wasn't wearing anything over his clothes, so his t-shirt clung to his muscles. She could easily see his six pack of abs. Damn.

"You think I'm crazy, but you ran out there without anything to protect yourself."

He glanced over at her with a smile, dimples and all.

"I never said *I* wasn't crazy."

They reached his house first.

"Why don't you come in for a cup of coffee?"

She should say no. Keeping her distance hadn't been hard, but it hadn't been easy either. And it hadn't helped one bit. She had been having dreams about both men. But, she'd barely talked to anyone in the last week, and she did like their company. Especially Mick. He was so easygoing and sweet.

"Sure, as long as Adam doesn't mind."

"He had a job today, so it's just me."

"Ah." That would be easier. Adam was nice, but he was always so intense.

She stepped through the door and immediately took off her shoes. He helped her off with her jacket. She immediately shivered.

"You need some coffee to warm up."

He led her to the kitchen. The boxes were gone, and the place was neat and orderly.

"Jeez, it took me forever to get settled in. I think I was unpacking months after moving. And you have a lot more things than I do."

"Military upbringing." He shrugged, then tugged off his shirt.

Good God in Heaven. She almost passed out from the

view in front of her. All tanned flesh, big muscles, and several tats. His skin was damp from the rain and she wanted to touch. Just run her hands over those enormous pecs...and lick at least one nipple.

Damn.

"Serenity?"

"Huh?"

"I'm going to get another shirt. I just started a pot when you went tearing off to the beach."

She nodded but she didn't move.

"Serenity?"

She blinked and finally focused on his face. He was smiling at her and there was a look in his eyes that told her he had picked up on her thoughts. Her face flamed.

"Cups are in the cupboard right above the coffee pot."

Then he disappeared to the back of the house. She drew in a deep breath and ordered each and every one of her hormones to settle down. When she was finally under control, she walked over to the coffee pot. She smiled when she saw every cup in perfect alignment.

"Military brat."

"And proud of it."

She jumped at the sound of his voice, then turned to face him. He had on another t-shirt and a new pair of shorts. His hair had been brushed back from his face, but with his fingers.

"Sorry. It's just so orderly."

He chuckled. "Yeah, there is that. No problem. I'm

proud of my military brat upbringing and the years I spent in the service."

"As you should be," she said with a smile.

"Everything has to be in perfect order for when my folks visit. It has more to do with my mother than my father, to tell you the truth."

He took the cup she held in her hands and poured coffee for her. "Milk? Sugar?"

She nodded and he went to retrieve them.

"Your mother is the task master?"

He nodded. "Always beware of the military mama. She's a dangerous creature."

She laughed enjoying him. It was nice to see a man who obviously loved his mother. "So, they visit?"

"Yeah, my parents and my sister come every now and then. She's hugely pregnant now, so I won't see her until the baby is born."

She doctored her coffee as he filled his cup.

"Take a load off," he said, motioning with his head. She walked into the living area. They had massive furniture that should have dwarfed the room, but somehow seemed to fit.

She sat down on the couch and he joined her on the opposite end.

"Is that what you do all the time? Run out in storms?"

She shook her head. "Not normally. But today was different. Plus, I'm working on a book."

"Oh? About Hawaii?"

She nodded. "I'm working on a proposal for a picture

book of Hawaii, but something different than what you find in other books. More of what is everyday life in Hawaii."

"Including big ass storms."

She smiled. "Yeah. I took some shots up at the North Shore also."

"Adam was working over there and is stuck taking the long way home more than likely. He said he was going to try and wait it out."

She nodded. "How long have you been together?"

"As in friends or lovers?"

"You were friends first?"

"Yes, we served together. We've been together as a couple for eight total."

She nodded. "Your folks don't have a problem with your homosexuality?"

He shook his head. "First, we aren't homosexual. We're both bisexual."

Oh, not good to hear. The fact that they liked each other and only other men worked for her. Granted, her dreams had moved from watching to being involved with them both. At the same time. But now she knew they liked women too, it was going to get worse.

"Ah."

"That doesn't bother you, does it?"

She shook her head. "I had a pretty liberal upbringing in LA. But your dad is retired military."

"My folks have never had a problem with it. Adam doesn't have a family to worry about."

She opened her mouth to ask why but the lights flickered then went out.

"Damn. Hold on."

He rose from the couch and started back into the kitchen. She heard a clunk, then, "Fuck, that's going to leave a mark. Gotta get used to the new house."

When he returned, he had a flashlight and a couple of candles.

He handed her the flashlight. Then he turned on the candles and set them on the table.

"Not very romantic, I know, but Adam has this thing about fires. Outside they don't bother him, but inside, he doesn't like them at all."

She nodded and turned off the flashlight.

"So, you are a photographer. Any family?"

She shook her head. "I have a mother I don't talk to."

"That's too bad."

She sipped at her coffee. "No. It's good. I emancipated myself at the age of sixteen. I haven't seen her since."

His eyes widened. "You could just do that? Walk away?"

"No, I was running. My mother was...is...a horrible person."

"Ah, okay. Adam had the same kind of thing. Foster kid."

She nodded. Some things were falling into place about the men. Mick came from a nurtured background. He was open and quick with a smile. Adam was guarded. Not rude, but he seemed to protect himself a little bit more.

"What did you do after you broke up with your mother?"

She smiled at the way he phrased it. "I traveled. I worked from the time I was five, so I had never really had a vacation."

"Wait, you worked?"

Damn. She didn't always tell people about her childhood. What was it about Mick that just made her spill her guts?

"Yeah. I was an actor."

He blinked. "Like on TV? You're famous?"

She snorted. "Not anymore and I don't think I was way back then either. Mainly smaller parts"

"I would have remembered an actress with the name Serenity Jones."

"I had a different name back then."

"Oh. Hmm. Still kind of hazy."

"Most of my shows and movies were geared toward girls."

"That would explain it. I bet my sister would know you."

She knew he wanted her stage name, but she didn't offer it. It was one thing she didn't want to deal with. Not when she barely knew them.

"So, you left the business."

She shrugged. "I was out of control. I hated acting, anything that had to deal with being in front of the camera. The two years before I left, I was completely out of control. I started drinking beer when I was twelve, wine when I was thirteen, then the harder stuff when I was fourteen. Lots of bad press, lots of recriminations."

She saw something pass over his face. "What?"

"You drank the other night."

She shook her head. "I could control it, I just didn't want to. When I left, I had been working for over a decade. I wanted to escape. After I left, I didn't drink until I was legal again and not that much."

"Ah. So, you emancipated yourself, changed your name, and ran away."

"Yeah. Pretty much." But now she wondered about what she had told him. She had only told a couple people about the book proposal. Now she had just blabbed about her other life.

"What's wrong?"

She looked up. "Sorry. I don't tell people about that all the time."

He nodded. "I'm almost a stranger and it's dark and stormy. Sometimes people let their guards down."

"I guess so."

"Don't worry. I won't tell anyone."

"I don't mind. I just don't want paparazzi to find me. It's been a decade but you never know."

"That's why you changed your name?"

"Yeah. And why I ran."

The old shame of her past crashed down on her hard. She knew it was the only thing she could do to save herself, but there were times she felt like a coward.

"Hey, I promise not to tell anyone."

"No. Just talking about it brings up a lot."

She looked down at her coffee cup.

"Like what?"

"My mother deemed me a coward for running. For walking away."

He slipped his finger beneath her chin and urged her to look at him.

"You are not a coward. I was pretty independent at that age, but I am not sure I could have walked out on my own. No family. That's pretty damned gutsy."

She smiled. "Thank you. I know all of that, but sometimes, it hits me."

He nodded.

"You're easy to talk to."

"I hear that a lot."

Even as she heard the change in his tone, she watched him lean forward. He brushed his mouth over hers. Not really a kiss, but she curled her toes against the bare floor.

When he pulled back, her lips were tingling. He dropped his hand.

"What was that for?"

"I thought you needed it."

She had, but...

"You're involved with Adam."

He nodded. "But we're open with our relationship."

"Listen, I don't want to get in between you two."

He chuckled. "Well..."

"What?"

He shook his head, his smile intact. With ease, he moved away from her and she instantly felt cold.

"No worries. I just wanted you to know that I'm interested."

"Hmm." It was the only thing she could say. Her body was still vibrating from the simple kiss. Something told her he knew exactly how to satisfy anyone—man or woman. It was in the way he moved. There was something so earthy and sexual.

"Hey, don't let it bother you. I was interested in Jillian at one time too, but she became one of our best friends."

She nodded. "And Adam doesn't mind this?"

"Adam was interested too."

She blinked. "What?"

He shook his head.

Irritation crept along her spine. She hated games. "No, you started this."

He sighed. "Adam is going to kill me. He told me to not say anything just yet."

"Say anything? You aren't making any sense."

"Adam and I like to share women."

Okay, again, she was born and raised in the dirtiest of cities, where people sold their souls and bodies for a chance at stardom. But even this shocked her. It happened and probably had at one of the parties she had been to. But, she had never had a person suggest it to her. What bothered her more was that she had been dreaming about it most nights.

"Share? As in taking turns."

He sipped his coffee, then shrugged. "Sometimes. Sometimes at the same time."

She said nothing again. Her brain had shifted into melt mode, and she wasn't sure if it was going to ever recover. It was as if he had been peeping into her secret dreams.

"But, if that's not your thing, then no worries, as I said before. Adam and I have quite a few female friends, and we would rather you be a friend than someone who avoids us."

Visions of Adam and Mick and what they could do to her flashed through her mind.

"I...listen, I'm usually not good with any kind of relationship. I find it hard to hold onto one guy. The idea that I would have to keep up with two is a little too much. Plus, I barely know you."

He nodded again. "Then get to know us. No pressure. If you change your mind, you let us know."

"Just like that?"

"Just like that." His voice was gentle.

"That makes me think you weren't really serious."

"How so?"

"If you were to give up that easily..." She let her words trail off, and she knew from the expression on his face that he understood.

"Listen, I want you. Actually, I've walked around half hard since I met you. Asking a woman to be shared by two men, especially after knowing them for a week, is odd. But know this, I would give anything to go down on you right now."

She blinked again. It was such plain talk, and she wasn't used to it.

"Uh."

Before he could respond, lights flashed through the window.

"Damn," Mick muttered.

"What?" she asked looking through the window.

"Adam. Listen, don't tell him I said anything."

"Why?"

"He wanted to wait."

"Jesus, you discussed this? Like a timeline?"

"Of course. And when I saw him with you the other night at dinner, I knew he was interested."

Before she could say anything, the front door opened, bringing with it Adam and rain.

"Mother fucker." Then he saw her on the couch. "Excuse my language."

Even as stunned as she was, she found the need to laugh about it.

"No problem."

Mick rose from the couch and easily crossed the floor and kissed Adam. "I thought you might hang out for a little longer."

"It wasn't that bad until I went through the tunnels on Pali. It's insane on the North Shore."

"Get some dry clothes on and we'll figure out dinner."

He nodded, giving Mick another kiss, then he headed to the back of the house. Dammit, why did she find that so damned hot? It was just a little kiss, but since the first time she had seen them, they had been turning her on.

"So, you want to stay for dinner?"

She sighed. "I shouldn't."

He smiled. "But you will."

He already knew her too well. She didn't know if that was a good or bad thing.

"You said get to know you. While I don't think I'll ever accept your proposition, I would like to know you better. The last neighbors were horrible, and you two are sweet."

He rolled his eyes. "Don't tell Adam."

"Don't tell Adam what?"

"I called you sweet."

He made a face. "We are not sweet."

Oh, God. He was so irritated it made her want to tease him even more.

"I invited her for dinner. I thought maybe some pasta," Mick said. Then he looked at her. "You're not one of those damned anti carbo freaks, are you?"

"I watch them, but I never turn down pasta when it's cooked by someone else."

"Great. I thought maybe a Pomodoro sauce would be good."

She glanced out the window. "It seems to have slowed down out there. I have a cabernet that would go great with that. Let me go pick it up and I'll be right back."

She grabbed her coat and slipped on her shoes.

"You don't have to do that," Adam said,

She smiled. "It's the least I can do. Mick gave me coffee and now he's cooking for me."

Not waiting for another argument from him, she rushed out the door. As she made her way over to her house, she couldn't get Mick's comments out of her head. She had been dreaming of them, thinking about what it would be like to have two men in her bed. Or theirs because hers was kind of small for all three of them.

Good God. No. Just dinner and some conversation with a nice Cab. Then she would come home. That was it.

SEVEN

Adam took a long pull off his longneck as he watched Mick work in the kitchen. As usual, he was humming while he cooked. Adam had never met another human being alive who liked to cook as much as Mick. It was a turn on to watch him move around the kitchen. Tonight, he was suspicious of his mood.

"So, what was going on when I got home?"

Mick glanced over his shoulder, then back to his work.

"We were talking."

"Talking?"

"Yep."

Irritation inched along his spine. He knew Mick answered in those short answers when he was trying to avoid the subject. Sometimes it was cute, but right now, it was getting on his last damned nerve.

"About what?"

Mick didn't answer, which had his suspicion soaring.

Dammit. What the hell had those two been brewing? Mick liked to muddy the waters. Adam walked over to the stove.

"Vincent McGrath."

Mick rolled his eyes. "Don't real name me."

"Well, I want an answer. What were the two of you doing?"

"Nothing, talking. I was getting to know her. I find her hot, but I also want to know her. Just like you do."

That much was true. "Did you find out anything interesting?"

He nodded. "She used to be a child star."

"Really?"

"Yeah. Under a different name. She didn't really want to talk about it. Or it felt like that to me, so I let it be."

"And now she's Serenity Jones."

"I think she changed her name for a lot of reasons, but one of them has to do with her mother. Not sure what happened, but she was emancipated when she was sixteen."

He settled back against the counter. "Interesting."

"I saw her heading to the beach when the rain started and followed her down. She's working on a book and wanted some shots of the storm."

"Seems like you were really chatty."

He glanced over at him. "Jealous?"

"No." Not really. "Just seems that you were talking to her a long time."

"You *were* jealous," Mick said as he set down the tongs. He stepped in front of Adam. Cupping his face, Mick leaned forward and brushed his mouth over Adam's.

"No reason to be jealous, since I told her about us."

"What?"

Mick smiled. "I thought I would let her know we're interested."

Anger surged. Always trying to push things too fast. "Dammit, Mick."

Mick sighed and moved away. Adam immediately felt guilty. Between the two of them, Mick was the dreamer. Adam was the pragmatist. That was why they made a great couple. It also meant that they always irritated each other.

"No worries," Mick said, as he salted the water and turned the burner on.

Adam sighed. "I'm sorry. I just don't want you to get your hopes up."

"I laid it out there. She knows, and I told her we wouldn't pressure her."

"Why?"

"What?"

"Why did you do that? Not your style. To tell her we would let her make the decision."

"Are you saying I'm pushy?"

"Yes."

Mick smiled at him, that little one that barely showed his dimples. Every. Damn. Time. All he had to do was smile at Adam, and Mick could talk him into anything.

"Ultimately, it will be her decision. We can't force her into a threesome. We aren't those kinds of guys. So, I thought it was best she knew we were interested in her. Being upfront also allows us to maintain a friendly relationship with her."

"How so?"

"If we sprung it on her later, she would say that is the only reason we wanted to be friends."

"But, we do want to be friends outside of that."

"Exactly. Still, she didn't freak out. She seemed intrigued."

"And that's your plan? Just throw it out there?"

"I said we wouldn't push, but we can entice."

He opened his mouth to respond, but there was a knock at the door.

"Hey," Serenity said through the screen door. She was smiling and dammit, it had the same effect on him that Mick's smile did. She pulled off her hood to reveal her hair. She'd brushed out her hair and left it in soft curls around her shoulders. He wanted to feel it on his flesh as she kissed her way down to his cock.

Damn.

"Sure, come in."

She pushed open the screen and took off her shoes, setting them beside both his and Mick's. Holding up the bottle of wine, she walked over to them.

"One of my favorite cabs."

He took it from her and looked at it. It was indeed a very good wine.

"Wow, that's..." Adam said, trailing off when she got close enough for him to smell the rain on her.

"What?" she asked.

"Well, almost too nice for the likes of us."

She laughed. "No way. I am so happy you're living here

66

after the last couple."

He set the wine on the counter and went to grab the wine cork.

"What was wrong with them?"

"They were in the middle of a divorce."

"That happens," Mick said.

She shook her head. "For three years. They both refused to move out. It was horrible."

"But you didn't move out?"

"I love my house. I refused to give in. I knew someday someone would move in I liked. And they did."

"How do you know that?" Adam asked.

"Mick is cooking for me and he made me coffee earlier. He is a prince among men. Plus, the only interaction I had with my last neighbors was from their attorneys."

"They were suing you?"

She chuckled. "No, they were each trying to get dirt on the other one for their divorce. If I thought it would work, I would have made up stuff. After observing them, I realized they just wanted to ruin each other's lives. It would have just drawn out the entire thing."

Adam concentrated on opening the wine and not the joy she brought to the kitchen. It wasn't something he could put his finger on, but she made everything somehow lighter.

"Did you get any good shots while you were taking your life for granted?" Mick asked.

"Yes, I did. And there were a lot of people on the beach."

"Haoles."

"No, most of those people were locals. We rarely get

waves like that on this beach. The photos are going to be stunning."

"So modest," Mick said.

"One thing I learned early in life is there is no room for false modesty. I'm a much better photographer than I was an actress."

"Yeah, Mick told me about that."

She made a face and shook her head. "It's nothing that big. Other than it gave me the ability to pursue my love of photography. I definitely didn't have any skills other than singing and acting; and, as I said, I wasn't that good at the latter."

"But singing."

"I'm okay. Nothing to write home about." She glanced at the stovetop. "That smells good."

"Mick has his mother's love of cooking and thankfully the ability."

"I can cook. But alone..."

Adam nodded. "Why bother. Yeah, Mick cooks like this so we can have leftovers if the other one is gone on a job."

"You two are crazy," Mick said with no heat. "I love to cook."

"I like to bake. I don't do it often, but when I do, I go to town."

"If you want to toss any of that over in our direction, we will gladly take it off your hands," Mick said. "I am not the best baker."

Adam snorted.

"What?" Serenity asked.

"It takes patience. Mick doesn't have much of that."

"You usually don't complain about that."

The change in Mick's tone told Adam he was talking about something else. Adam just smiled, then turned to pull down the wine glasses.

"So, how about we leave him in the kitchen and drink some of this wine in the living room?" Adam asked.

"Sure," Serenity said.

The vibe she was giving off was that she was open to the idea of sex with them. He needed to get to know her better, and besides, getting time alone with Serenity was not a bad thing.

———

BY THE END OF THE NIGHT, SERENITY'S HORMONES were singing. She knew that neither of the guys had picked up on it. Maybe she was a better actress than she thought.

Also, she had drunk a lot, so that had smoothed out her nerves a bit. She wasn't a heavy drinker anymore, so just a few glasses went to her head.

"Take this," Mick said as he handed her a container with leftover pasta. "We're out a lot this coming week on jobs, so it will just go to waste here."

"Thank you. I need to hit the farmers market and Food-land, but I got distracted today."

His mouth curved. "Yeah."

"Mick," Adam said, the warning easy to hear in his voice.

"What?"

She glanced at Adam and knew then that they had talked about it already.

"You promised you wouldn't pressure me."

"I'm not pressuring you. I'm just agreeing," Mick said.

She looked at Adam, who rolled his eyes. "Mick is just a flirt. It has nothing to do with anything else. It's his father in him."

"I just don't want you to think I'm teasing you. I am not someone who easily gets involved with men in general, so this would be unprecedented."

"No worries. I'll control him."

Before she knew what Adam was going to do, he leaned forward and brushed his mouth over hers. "Thank you for sharing a meal with us."

"Yes, thank you," Mick said, giving her an easy kiss. "We really enjoyed having you."

"Thank you. It's nice to eat with other people. I eat alone a lot and I like it, but conversation is good sometimes too." She slipped on her sandals. "Goodnight."

"Goodnight," they said in almost stereo precision. She walked down the stairs and then hurried along the path to her house. She unlocked her door then glanced over her shoulder. The guys were standing there watching her.

She waved to let them know she was okay, then she stepped into her house. She shut the door and slipped off her sandals. After putting the pasta in her fridge, she poured a glass of water and thought about her new neighbors.

They were both super sweet. Oh, Adam tried to play the stoic Alpha, but she suspected he had a soft center. She saw it tonight when he talked to Mick. And Mick. She smiled. He was the biggest flirt, but again, she suspected there was more to his personality.

It had been so long since anyone had worried about her. She'd been on her own for over ten years, and even before that, her mother didn't truly care about her. She cared about the money Kayleigh Rose could make. But the guys, they had watched out for her. The path from their house to hers was just a few yards. They stood there looking out for her. A smile curved her lips and warmth filled her.

It was nice to have someone who cared about you.

eight

Adam stepped out of the shower and had just began to towel off when someone knocked at his door. He wrapped the towel around his waist and walked to the door. When he saw Serenity standing on the other side, he smiled.

It had been two weeks since the dinner they had shared, and he was getting worse than Mick. He found ways to run into her on a regular basis. If she figured it out, she didn't say anything. It was already beyond mortifying. That shame would only increase if she knew about it.

Her back was to him, so he took his time to look at her. She had her blond curls up in a ponytail, giving him an excellent view of her neck. He had a thing for slender necks. He liked to graze his teeth across the tender skin as he rode a woman from behind.

She turned at that moment and he was thankful he hadn't opened the door. She offered him a sunny smile and he realized she was holding a box. He ordered his body to settle down and then opened the door.

"Hey, there," she said, after he finally opened the door. Then, her gaze travelled down his torso and he knew he was still damp from his shower. Dammit, if she kept looking at him that way, he wasn't going to be able to fight off his erection. There would be no hiding it behind his towel. He was a Dom and could control himself, to a point. And that point was apparently the woman standing in front of him.

"Hey, yourself. Did you buy me a gift?"

For a second, she said nothing, then the most delightful blush colored her cheeks. Damn, she was cute.

"Uh...no. Oh, the box." She handed it over to him. "They left it with me, on account that I saw them trying to leave it on your lanai and I marched over here and got it."

He chuckled and glanced at the name. It was Mick's and one of their favorite stores to buy gear at. He didn't need a vivid imagination to figure out who Mick bought toys for.

"Thanks."

"Because, you know, there are a lot of tourists around, and you never know what they are going to do. So, that's why I did it."

"Okay. Did you want to come in?"

"Uh?" her gaze drifted down his torso once again.

"I can throw on some clothes--"

"Oh, no don't do that." She closed her eyes and muttered something under her breath. "What I meant was that I need to get back to work, and I'm going out tonight."

"Hot date?"

She snorted. "Not likely. I'm doing some nighttime shoots tonight."

Her tongue darted out and wet her lips. The woman was going to kill him.

"I should go. Yeah. See you later."

She hurried down the steps and onto the path that led to her house before he could even say goodbye. He watched her until she disappeared into her house, then he shut his front door. Lord only knew what Mick ordered, but Adam was damned glad he had now.

SERENITY SLAMMED HER DOOR SHUT AND LEANED back against it. Her skin was flushed, and her body lit up like some kind of bingo machine. Sex bingo. That is what it felt like.

For two weeks she had tried to stay away, but today, she made the effort to be neighborly, and see what happened?

"No. Just have to be some stupid donkey Girl Scout and run over there to save their package."

She snorted.

"Like anyone really comes through here."

But she worried about it. And see what it got her? Hot and bothered and no way to relieve the sexual tension.

There's a way, a naughty little voice whispered inside of her.

"Shut up."

No. Two hot guys want to do you, but you are living like a nun.

She rolled her eyes. Serenity stopped listening to the bad voice years ago. It had gotten her in too much trouble, and that's what those men were. They were sweet, but they were also trouble. For her sanity, mainly. What woman would just take up with two gorgeous men who wanted to give her pleasure?

A very smart woman.

"Go away."

Great, now they had her talking to her voice again. That was a really bad sign. But then, any kind of romantic or sexual relationship had always been hard for her.

Dealing with one man was too much, so she was fairly certain she wouldn't have the emotional capacity to deal with two of them. She'd spent years trying to figure out why men seemed to run from her, or vice versa.

Emotionally distant.

It was a term everyone used for her. Her shrink, several exes, her mother. She made a face. No need to bring Broomhelda into her thoughts today. Not when she had the pleasure of seeing one of the finest male specimens she had seen in a long, long while.

God, he was gorgeous. All sinewy muscle, and tats. He had tats like Mick. Then that little happy trail of hair that disappeared beneath the towel...she was humming. With her voice, but also her body. She had wanted to do nothing more than to lean forward and lick one of those droplets of water that clung to his flesh. His gorgeous, golden flesh.

Damn. She needed to get out of here before she made an ass out of herself. Mainly because that stupid voice was trying to get her to go back over to Adam and beg him to do her. Like all kinds of doing. It had been a long time since she had thought about that, or at least, thought about that with a man.

She would go and do her shoot and work it out of her system. She'd been horny before and dealt with it. She would deal with it now.

MICK STEPPED OUT OF HIS TRUCK WHEN HE SAW Serenity coming out of her house. She was carrying a camera bag as she hurried to her car.

"Hey," he called out. She glanced over and gave him a smile, but it wasn't one of her grins. He had gotten used to those. This one was strained, and she looked like she wanted to avoid him.

He walked over as she put her bag in the backseat. When she did, her cut offs moved up and gave him a better view of her ass. She wasn't skinny and he liked a woman with a full, round ass. It was so nice to spank.

"Out for a shoot tonight?"

She started as if she hadn't known he had come over.

"Sorry. Didn't mean to scare you."

She shook her head. "Just a little stressed today. And how did you know I was going for a shoot?"

"That's your camera bag, right?"

She turned around and looked back over her shoulder. She sighed. "Yes."

She was looking everywhere but at him. Even after he had told her about Adam and him wanting her, she had looked him in the eye. Something happened.

"Are you okay?"

She nodded and crossed her arms beneath her breasts. Every one of her physical ques told him to stand back. It was odd. From the moment he had met her, she had been welcoming. Even after he told her both he and Adam wanted her, she hadn't acted like this. Now, she was standoffish, as if she was afraid he would jump her.

"Okay, I guess I will let you go. Be careful."

"I will."

Then she got in her car and drove away. He watched until she turned onto the highway. Mick knew he wasn't wrong. She was out of sorts and it had something to do with him. As he turned and made his way to the house, his gaze settled on Adam's truck. Dammit.

He hurried up the steps and into the house.

"Just what the hell did you do?"

Adam, who had been cutting up veggies to grill looked up at him.

"Well, hello lover. Nice to see you too."

He rolled his eyes. "Hello. Now tell me what you did to her."

"Her?"

"Serenity."

"Nothing. She did bring over this package."

78

He nudged a box on the counter.

"Great. I was hoping these would come soon," Mick said picking them up.

"What did you buy?"

"A few things just in case."

"Ah."

"So, what did you do that upset her?"

"I did nothing."

"Nothing? Tell me what happened."

"I was taking a shower and was just drying off when she knocked on the door. I wrapped the towel around my waist and answered the door."

"You mean you answered the door naked?"

"No. I was wearing a towel."

Mick rolled his eyes. He loved Adam but the man was obtuse about his effect on people. Built like a MAC truck, with tattoos and golden skin, the man was the epitome of a beach volleyball player. All that sun-streaked hair helped complete the picture.

"And?"

"And nothing." He shrugged and picked up the plate and then grabbed the tongs. Then, just as if they weren't having a conversation, he walked out of the kitchen toward the back of the house.

There was a good chance Mick could get off for justifiable homicide. Grumbling, he followed Adam out onto the back lanai.

"It isn't nothing," Mick said. "She wouldn't look me in the eye."

"Maybe she thinks your eyes are ugly."

"My eyes aren't ugly and you damned well know it."

Mick didn't miss the curve of Adam's lips. It was that half smile that always got to him. Fuck.

"Adam."

He laughed. "Sorry, it was too much fun. But I do think our very lovely Ms. Jones is not as immune to us as she presents herself to be."

"Why do you say that?"

"She couldn't stop looking at my chest and she kept forgetting what she meant to say."

"Yeah?" he asked, his mood quickly changing.

"Oh, yeah. She's attracted to both of us, but I don't know if she's interested in what you proposed to her."

"But definitely attracted?"

He nodded.

"Attraction is just one step. Now, we need to send out feelers again."

"Give it a break, Mick. God, you act like it's a military campaign. Just let it happen. You have a perfectly acceptable sexy companion for the night."

Mick slipped his hands around Adam's waist and kissed his neck. "There is that."

"Was any of that stuff in the box for either of us?"

"Not really. Well, they would be for us to use."

He lifted a carrot to his mouth and Mick took it easily. "With Ms. Jones?"

He nodded. "Yeah."

"Then I hope she takes a chance."

"She will."

His grunt told Mick he wasn't so sure of it.

"I need to get cleaned up and I'll help with dinner."

Adam gave him a kiss on the cheek before Mick moved away. As he stripped his clothes off, he thought of Serenity and the need they both had for her. It was starting to become an obsession for him, and that was not a good thing. Still, he knew she was close to granting them their request. And if she did take that chance, it was going to be one of the sweetest things he'd ever experienced.

nine

B y the time Serenity returned home that night, her nerves were a jangled mess. Because she was an early riser, she had caffeinated herself to keep alert during the shoot. She had enjoyed it. Nighttime wasn't one of the most popular images to sell of Hawaii. People wanted sun, sand, and seduction. But, there was something about Hawaii at nighttime. The air was at its sweetest, less humid, and it clung to her. It was one of the things she loved about Hawaii, so she wanted to include it in her book. She'd taken the regular pics of the lighthouse and the beach at night. Then, she had driven out to the North Shore to get pictures of the moon dancing over the waves.

With all the driving, she had to make sure she stayed alert. The problem with that was that Adam had her entire body purring like a well-loved cat. Granted, other than that simple kiss a few weeks ago, neither man had made advances. She appreciated it. Now though, she was paying for it. More than likely, she was going to spend the night with her battery-operated boyfriend.

She parked in front of her house and tried not to look over at their house. If she did, and they were awake, she would be tempted to go over there. Just to chat. Just to...

Dammit. She didn't need this complication in her life. She had made it worse by reading a few ménage romance books, and then the inevitable porn search. She knew how all the particulars worked, but it wasn't something she had looked for before now. Now, she was obsessing about it. It had been a problem for her most of her life. Every shrink she had had over the years said the same thing. Her obsession over subjects tended to blur her focus. Up until she had walked away from the mess of her life ten years earlier, men had always been the ones to fill that slot. And, now there were two of them who were occupying her thoughts.

She grabbed her camera back when she heard steps behind her. Dammit. She didn't know if she could resist their invitation tonight. Not when her body wanted to betray her.

"Hey," Adam said. She glanced over her shoulder and saw that it was both men. They were going to double team her.

Dammit. Now she had that thought in her head and the double entendre it created. Worse, they were both wearing hardly any clothing. Both were wearing tank tops. Even in the darkness she could make out the sculpted muscles both men sported. Or had she just memorized exactly how they looked?

God, she needed help.

"Hey," she said.

"We were a little worried about you."

She frowned. "Why?"

"It's late and you were by yourself."

"Believe me, I know how to handle myself. I don't need a bodyguard."

The men shared a glance. There was some kind of silent communication between them.

"Yeah, but you're our friend and we worry about you," Mick said.

It was dark but she could see the sincerity in his gaze. She nodded. "Sorry. I'm just not good company now."

"Is there something wrong?"

"Something wrong? Naw. I just have you two standing there with tank tops on and board shorts like some kind of surfer wet dream."

Another shared glance. She ground her teeth.

"And stop that."

Adam's eyebrows raised up. "Do what?"

"That silent communication thing."

He opened his mouth but she plowed ahead. "I was up at five this morning and I need to get to bed. I'm exhausted."

They both nodded.

"Oh, good lord, stop being so accommodating." Silence greeted that comment. "What? What is it that you two get by coming over here?"

Mick tilted his head to the side and studied her. "Get what?"

"Apparently, it's a woman yelling at us," Mick said.

"I am not yelling!" Then she realized she was. Dammit. Mick snorted.

"I just need to go to bed."

"I'm okay with that," Mick said.

"No. I need rest. In bed. Away from you. Far away from both of you."

With that, she marched up her front steps, and unlocked her front door. She knew they were back there, but she continued to ignore them when she slammed the door shut.

If her nerves had been jangled before, they were tornado sirens now, screeching and annoying. It was all their fault. She had been happy to live in her little house by the water, away from the limelight and pressures she had dealt with during her childhood and adolescence.

She heard the creak on her front lanai. "Are you sure you're okay, Serenity?" Mick asked.

She closed her eyes as embarrassment stole over her.

"Yes. Just tired."

"Okay. Text us if you need to."

"Good night, Serenity," Adam said.

"Goodnight, guys."

Then, she heard them walk down the steps.

"I'M JUST SAYING THAT SHE IS DEFINITELY thinking about it."

Adam ground his teeth together as he turned off Kam Highway onto the street that lead to their house.

"Yeah, that was pretty obvious."

"Exactly. I think we should invite her over for dinner again."

"Just let it go."

"What?"

"I just wish you would quit talking about it."

"I can't, because if I stop talking, then I start thinking about it, and man o man those are some bad thoughts."

As he turned onto the little driveway they shared with Serenity, Adam's heartbeat increased. Damn, his palms were sweaty. The woman was driving him insane and she probably didn't even know it. And, as Mick continued to drone on about her and her feelings, his cock was coming up with its own ideas.

She was standing on their lanai when they pulled up. She turned when she heard them drive up. She smiled, but it wasn't one of those sunny smiles. Instead, it was guarded. He hated that. He didn't want her to think she had to hide her feelings from him.

"What do you think she wants?" Mick asked.

He shrugged, but said nothing. Mick was already slipping out of the truck.

"Sorry, I thought someone was home because Mick's truck was here," Serenity said.

"We were working the same job today, so we rode in together," Mick said.

He could barely hear them because he was still sitting in the truck like an idiot.

"Are you going to join us?" Mick asked.

Adam didn't respond. It was hard to talk around the lump in his throat. He grabbed his gun and slipped out of the truck. It was then that he noticed she was holding what looked like the mac bread she had brought over when they first moved in.

"I just wanted to apologize for last night."

Mick glanced at him, then looked back at Serenity.

"There's nothing to apologize for."

She opened her mouth to argue, but Adam wanted to have this conversation in private.

"Let's go inside and talk about it."

"No, really. I just wanted to drop this off."

He heard the fine sheen of arousal in her voice. She wanted them, wanted to experiment. But she was a little wary.

"We promise not to bite," Adam said.

She sighed. "I can't promise that on my end."

His libido went into overdrive.

"Yeah?" Mick said. "Then you definitely need to come in."

She was wavering, it was easy to see. She looked to Adam.

"That's a good idea. Hands off unless you want differently."

"Okay."

Mick smiled at him and walked up the stairs to the lanai. As he unlocked the door, Serenity continued to look at him as if she were waiting for him to say something. Again, he wasn't able to speak, because at the moment, he was overwhelmed. This woman was gorgeous, that much was true.

But there was a true light within her that was easy to see. And it drew him like a June bug to a light.

As soon as Mick had the door opened, she turned and walked in. Damn, she was going to kill him with those cutoffs.

He followed the other two through the door. He set his gun down on the counter.

"Give me a sec," Mick said as he grabbed Adam's gun. He knew he was going to put them in their side table drawers.

Alone with Serenity. Damn.

It only took a few seconds for Mick to return, but it seemed like a lifetime. She continued to stare at him with those amazing whiskey-colored eyes.

"I will happily take the offering," Mick said, taking the bread from her.

"Oh," she said, the look on her face told Adam that she'd forgotten she was holding it.

"Now, tell us why you must apologize," Mick said.

Her tongue darted out over her full lower lip and Adam groaned.

"What?" she asked.

"Nothing," he said shaking his head.

"Tell us," Mick insisted.

Her eyes widened and for good reason. Mick seemed easy going, but he was a Dom and that was his Dom voice. It was what made him so damned irresistible. The two sides of the coin.

"I-I..."

"Mick," Adam said. "Give her a little space."

Mick made a face and took a step back. He sometimes forgot how intimidating he could be. Adam looked at Serenity.

"Now, tell us. Why should you apologize when you were just being truthful?"

"I think it's a bad habit. No. I know it's a bad habit."

"What is? Apologizing for your feelings?"

"No, for taking out my feelings on someone else."

He shared a knowing look with Mick and he nodded. He was going to be the one who did the talking right now.

"And stop that."

"What?" Adam asked.

"That silent communication you two do. It is a little disconcerting. I told you that last night."

He almost looked at Mick but stopped himself. "Sorry. I think it's just habit. We've been together for so long. We work in the field a lot, so it's just something that helps. And when we're playing, we often share the role of Dom."

"Oh, yeah, forgot about that. I don't do that."

"And you don't have to," Mick said. "If you were interested in learning, we would be happy to teach you. It adds another level to lovemaking, but it isn't something we have to have."

Adam almost rolled his eyes. He knew Mick had bought toys just for her, so he was going to use everything in his arsenal to get her to experiment.

"I don't know," she said.

"Why don't we just try to play a little? A little kissing,

then see where it goes from there. You say stop, we stop," Mick offered as he looked at Adam. "Right?"

He nodded, trying to keep his brain focused on the question, but he was too busy creating more fantasies in his head. He knew that there was always a chance she would stop them and push them away. And it had never really bothered him in the past, but with this woman, it felt somehow different.

"So, what do you say, Serenity?" Mick asked.

She studied Mick then she looked at Adam. She was still, almost as if she wasn't breathing, but Adam could sense the inner turmoil raging inside of her. It wasn't an easy thing to decide, especially for a woman who had only known them for a month.

"And you want this?" she asked.

He could only answer her honestly.

"Almost more than my next breath."

Her expression lightened. And something close to relief flited through his system. Just that little lift in her spirits made his heart happy.

"Then my answer is yes."

ten

For a long second, Mick wasn't sure he had heard her right. He glanced at Adam, who smiled at him, and they both looked at her.

Her eyes widened. "Oh, no. I'm not sure I like *that* look."

Mick laughed and started toward her. She squeaked and stepped back, but Mick didn't stop his forward progression.

"Mick," she said. Her stern look made him think she was trying to take control of the situation. Unfortunately for Serenity, her voice came out all breathless.

He picked her up and she squeaked again, apparently not ready for the move.

"You'll learn that is a very *good* look for both of us to have. It means we are going to do some filthy things to you."

Her eyes widened again as she looked over his shoulder at Adam. Knowing his lover the way Mick did, Adam just nodded.

"In here or the bedroom?" he asked, his voice hoarse even

to his own ears. It hadn't been that long since they'd met her, but each day his need for her had been building to monumental proportions.

When she didn't answer him, he realized she wasn't sure if he was talking to her.

"Serenity, your choice."

She looked back at him, and said, "I think the bedroom."

He continued to carry her down the hallway, with Adam following them.

"I have two legs and can walk."

"Yeah, but it's nice to have a little help every now and then. Plus, I like carrying you."

"How could you possibly know that before now?"

Instead of answering, he laughed and kissed her. He was just too damned happy to fight her on something like that. He stepped into the bedroom and she looked at the bed. It was a California King, and one of their prized possessions.

"Good God," she said, her voice seemingly breathless. "You could have an orgy on that thing."

"Nope, just a ménage," Adam said as he walked past them.

"I'm amazed this room is so big."

"It's one of the reasons we wanted the house. We need room for sleep...and other things."

"Put her down," Adam said.

He didn't object. They shared being Dom, but there was always a lead. Tonight, it apparently was going to be Adam, even though they weren't playing. One of them had to be in charge or it could get awkward.

He did as Adam instructed, letting her slide down the length of his body. There was no way she could mistake the bulge in his pants. She shivered as her feet hit the floor. Just that little gesture had his body singing. He couldn't wait to see all her reactions when they made love to her.

She stood before them. "What now?"

Instead of answering, Mick leaned forward to kiss her. She shuddered, and opened her mouth in invitation. He took advantage of the offer and plunged his tongue inside her mouth. A low growl vibrated in his chest, his need to dominate clawed to take control, but he beat it back. It wouldn't do to scare her, not when they finally got her to agree to this. His heartrate soared as she raised herself to her tiptoes to meet his demand. She might have been a little leery, but that had vanished. She pressed her body against his, her hardened nipples easy to feel through their layers of clothing.

He pulled back and Adam stepped up for a taste. Mick watched, finding the scene in front of him arousing. Adam slanted his mouth over hers as his hands traveled to her ass. Watching his lover's hands caress her as he urged her closer had pushed Mick's arousal a little higher. This was always part of the excitement of ménages for him. He loved to watch Adam touch a woman, give her pleasure. It added another layer to the hunger they were building. Mick was sure it was the same for Adam.

She moaned, the sound of it music to his ears. Adam gave her tongue one long suck, then pulled back.

"So, you still with us?"

Her eyes fluttered open as her tongue slipped out over

her lips. He knew it was a nervous gesture, but he fantasized that she could taste him and Adam there.

"Oh, yeah."

AROUSAL DEEPENED HER VOICE AND VIBRATED over his soul. This woman, this time, it was more important than every other time before.

"Let's get a little more comfortable."

She nodded as Adam peeled off her shirt and Mick made quick work of her jean shorts. She wasn't wearing a bra, so she stood in front of them with nothing on but a black thong.

Neither one of them said a word. Mick couldn't because his brain just wouldn't function. Soft flesh kissed by the sun, full breasts, and a body that was fit but also not overly hard. His mouth went dry as he continued to stare at her.

"You're making me nervous," she said. It took him a full ten seconds to move his gaze away from her breasts and back to her face.

"Why would you be nervous?" Adam asked.

She snorted. "I don't think either of you have any idea the effect you have on people. Both of you are standing there, fully clothed, and looking me over."

They led her to the bed and then joined her. Adam said nothing, but he positioned himself lower. Mick watched as Adam set a hand on each of her knees, then he slowly spread them apart. Mick moved, so he could get a better view. Adam's position left him eye level to Serenity's breasts.

Adam leaned forward and teased her nipple with the tip of his tongue before taking it fully into his mouth. Serenity moaned and speared her fingers through his hair, then molded her hands to his head. Not wanting to be left out, Mick stepped closer. He threaded his hands through her hair. A little harsher than he had meant to, he tugged her head back. He leaned down, and took her mouth. Wet, hot, and thoroughly breathtaking. The woman knew how to kiss. He couldn't wait to feel her talented lips wrap around his cock.

She reached out with her hand to trail over the hard ridge in his board shorts. As she teased him with her fingers, Mick sensed Adam moving down her body. He pulled away from Serenity's mouth to watch Adam's head as he kissed his way down her belly. With practiced ease, Adam slipped her thong off and threw it behind him to the floor. Mick almost laughed because Adam was such a stickler for neatness, but with Serenity, he apparently didn't care. He could certainly understand the feeling.

Adam buried his head between her legs, just as she slipped her hand beneath the waistband of his shorts. She wrapped her hand around his cock and gave it a gentle squeeze.

He sucked in a breath. She looked up at him through her lashes, a devilish smile curving her lips. Easing his shorts down, she leaned forward and circled the head of his penis with her tongue. He shuddered.

"Oh, you like that?" she asked. She opened her mouth to say something else, but Adam pressed a finger inside of her. She gasped and spread her legs wider. "God."

As Adam continued to tease her, she pulled herself together and turned her attention to Mick. She took him fully into her mouth as she slipped her hand between his legs to scrape her fingers over his sac. Shit. He almost came right there and then. She was taking him deeper and deeper into her mouth, when Adam growled. He gave her pussy one last lick then he stood up. He cupped the back of Mick's neck and pulled him over for a long, wet kiss. He could taste her on Adam's tongue, the musky flavor of her arousal danced over his taste buds. When Adam pulled back, he looked down at Serenity, who was still sucking on his cock.

"Fuck," Adam said.

"You have no idea," he ground out.

Adam slipped off his shorts and shirt, then grabbed a condom.

"Come on, you two," he said, humor lacing his voice as Serenity continued to take Mick into her mouth. One last suck and he pulled away. Her eyes fluttered open just as Adam reached around him for the anal plug he'd bought for her. After applying some lube, he handed it to Mick.

"What's that?" she asked, excitement and weariness filling her voice.

"It's an anal plug. We'd like to take you at the same time, but you aren't ready."

She shivered, her breasts swaying with the movement. Adam grabbed her nipple and pinched it. Her excited gasp told Mick she was definitely up for a little play.

Without a word, Adam leaned down, took her by the waist and turned her over onto her stomach.

"Up on your knees."

She did as instructed and Adam made a gesture for Mick to insert the plug.

"This is so we can both take you at some point. I'm assuming you haven't had much anal sex," Mick said.

"None."

Adam nodded as if she confirmed his suspicions. "Just relax. It won't hurt," he said as he sat on the bed in front of her. He cupped her face. "If it does, you just tell us no. You control this."

She nodded and Adam brushed his mouth over hers. When he pulled back, Mick pressed the plug into her ass. He took it slowly, knowing this was her first time. Still, as he eased it in she moaned.

"That doesn't hurt, does it?"

"No."

"If it does, you tell us. This isn't about pain. It's all about pleasure."

She nodded at Adam. His hardened cock bobbed up against his abs and Mick couldn't hold it in. He had to sigh.

"My thoughts exactly," Serenity said.

He glanced at her and she was smiling back at him. She hadn't moved from her position and it struck him that she was going to be a fun sub to play with. She might not under-stand it right now, but she was perfect for play in the bedroom. He gave her ass a light spank. She gasped but she wiggled her ass. Yeah, she was going to be perfect.

Adam had grabbed a condom and was about to open it when Mick slid off the bed and took the package from him.

"What?" he asked, but from the tone in his voice, he knew what Mick had planned.

After ripping the package open, he slipped the condom out and placed it on the head of Adam's cock. Then, without breaking eye contact. Inch by inch, he teased his lover, letting his fingers skim the bare skin before the latex rolled over the flesh.

Adam leaned his head back and groaned.

"Fuck."

"Yeah," Mick said as he leaned forward and licked Adam's neck, then leaned closer and kissed him.

When he pulled back, both men were breathing heavily.

"Oh, my," Serenity said. They turned their heads. She was still there on the bed where they had ordered her to stay.

"Like what you see, Serenity?" Mick asked.

She nodded, as her gaze rose to theirs. "Definitely."

Mick didn't have to be told what to do next. He climbed up on the bed in front of her as Adam did the same behind her.

Serenity licked her lips.

"Oh, she's hungry for a taste of cock, aren't you?"

She nodded, but didn't take her gaze from his cock.

He held it up for her and she eagerly opened her mouth. The wet warmth surrounded his flesh. He started to thrust in and out of her mouth, as Adam entered her from behind. She moaned against his cock, the vibrations dancing over his flesh.

She arched her back as Adam thrust harder and harder into her. Soon she was working in rhythm of Adam's thrusts.

Each time Adam plunged into her pussy, she took Mick into her mouth. That hot, wet mouth and the fucking talented tongue. She wrapped it around his shaft as she hummed. She was going to kill him. Over and over, she slid her tongue over him, sucking him so hard at times, he was sure he'd come before he wanted to.

Then, she upped her game. Sliding her hand up his thigh to his sac. She teased him, sliding her fingers over it before cupping it completely. The soft, gentle touch had his head spinning and just about all thoughts of holding back for his orgasm dissolving. Another long hum from her and he thrust into her mouth one last time and let his orgasm take over. All the tension over these last few weeks released. He couldn't stop the long, loud groan that vibrated from deep in his soul. Serenity didn't hesitate. She sucked him harder and longer than before, lapping up all of his cum and prolonging his pleasure.

When she was done, he leaned down, cupped her chin, and kissed her.

"Thank you."

She had no time to respond. He moved out of the way as Adam reached down, pulling her upright. Mick watched mesmerized as Adam fucked her so hard the entire bed was moving. She was beautiful, her body slick with sweat. Her moans grew louder as Adam's rhythm ramped up.

"Fuck, yes, fuck," was all Adam ground out, punctuating each thrust. Mick reached out and pinched her nipples, then slipped his hand down to her clit. She was so fucking wet.

"Serenity," Mick said. It took some effort, but her eyes finally opened. "Come."

Mick pressed her clit—once, twice—and she went flying over. Her body shook with the force of the orgasm. Her scream was filled with both surprise and relief. She jolted against Adam, who had continued to plunge in and out of her pussy. One last hard thrust and Adam came as he shouted Serenity's name. He released her and she fell forward onto the bed. Mick leaned over to kiss Adam. Then, he moved out of the way. Adam pulled out of Serenity and settled beside her. For a long moment, Mick stared at the two of them cuddled together.

Something shifted in his chest and he rubbed his hand over it. This was what he wanted. All three of them together. Forever.

He knew they both would probably tell him it was too fast. He knew for a fact that Adam would. But this was it. What he wanted and, in part, what all three of them needed.

"Are you just going to stand there and stare at us?" Serenity asked.

Adam lifted his head from the pillow, his eyes barely opened.

"Come on, Mick. Stop thinking."

He smiled and did just as Adam said. Worry would come later. With that thought, he laid down beside Serenity, slipping his arm over both Adam and Serenity.

Yes, he thought as he started to drift off to sleep. This was exactly what they all needed.

eleven

Serenity awoke to the slant of sun across her eyes. She frowned, keeping her eyes closed, trying to think of why that would happen. Her bedroom faced the west. When she thought she would be able to take the sun, she opened her eyes.

This was not her bed, or her house. Of course, it wasn't her bed. It wasn't like someone would break into her house and leave a massive bed. She pulled herself up to her elbows and looked around.

Adam and Mick's bedroom. And she was alone. How is it that she went to bed with two men and still found herself alone?

Jesus. She collapsed onto the bed as memories of the previous night came rushing back to her. She'd slept with two men...at the same time. Who did that kind of thing? Apparently, she did.

She closed her eyes. It had never been a fantasy of hers to

have two men simultaneously. As she had thought before, she couldn't handle *one* man all that well. Her relationships had either been volatile or boring. Lately, they had been non-existent. It wasn't that she shunned men, but she didn't have a reason to venture out.

Now that wasn't true. She had avoided fixups from the few friends she had on the island. She just didn't have the time or energy for a relationship.

Once she'd stepped into that arena, she had picked *two* men. Good God, her last shrink was right. She set herself up for failure every time. How was this even supposed to work? And, all of her reasons for doing it had flown out the window just because they made her hot.

She opened her eyes and stared at the ceiling. It was hard to feel badly about the sex, but a relationship was out of the question. She lived right next door. When it ended--and all of her relationships did--it would be awkward.

She sat up and looked around the room. She didn't want to get dressed back into her clothes. If she was going to have only one night with these men, she wanted to stay naked as much as possible.

She spotted a blue dress shirt. Slipping out of bed, she grabbed it and headed to the bathroom.

After turning on the light, she stared at herself in the mirror. Jesus. She had whisker burn all over her body, little splotches of red that revealed to her every part of her body they had kissed, licked, and tasted.

She shivered. Just the memory of the lovemaking had her body revving up for another round. God, what was she going to do? They tempted her into believing they could just play and have fun. But consequences always came with daylight, and she knew in the morning it would be hard to pretend this was about having fun. It was most definitely that, but she was already growing attached. Hell, she had been growing attached since they showed up at her door begging for more bread. They were just so sweet and adorable. She smiled thinking about how Adam didn't like to be called sweet.

Her smile faded. Dammit, she *was* already attached. Worse, they didn't need her. They were a couple who had been together for years. They had each other.

With a sigh, she set the shirt on the counter. After relieving herself, she slipped the shirt on and went in search of the guys.

She heard the rumble of male voices in the kitchen and followed the sound. She knew it was wrong, but she stood just out of sight so she could hear the conversation.

"Come on, Mick. You know women don't go for that kind of thing. They don't want to be a third in a relationship. Especially with two guys who have been committed to each other as long as we have."

She frowned. It wasn't something she thought of, at least not until recently, but she knew Adam was right. Most women didn't want to be a third wheel. They liked to be the center of attention. Although, last night, she was exactly that. Having two men focus just on her was something that she had never had and, dammit, it was exhilarating. It was also addicting, which might be an issue.

"But if she wanted to, you would be open to it?" Mick asked.

There was no noise, but from Mick's next response, Serenity assumed that Adam nodded.

"See."

"There is no *see*. We also have another side to our bed play with women. You haven't even approached her about that."

Another side?

"Come on. You saw her last night. She liked being told what to do. She kneeled on the bed without having to be ordered. Fucking sexy."

"We still have to talk to her about it."

"It isn't something you can slip into casual conversation," Mick said.

"That never stopped you before."

Mick snorted. "We'll never know unless we ask.

"True, but if you ask too early, we might frighten her off."

Adam was talking about her like she was a little scaredy cat. She had heard enough. She stepped into the kitchen. They were sitting at the counter, each had a cup of coffee in front of them.

Neither of them noticed her to begin with, and she was glad for it. It gave her time to look them over. Both were wearing jean shorts and nothing else. In fact, she was sure Mick's shorts weren't even buttoned.

As Adam moved, she watched the ripple of muscle in his back and had to bite back a sigh. Mick wasn't any better. He stretched his hands over his head. Oh, God. How did she land these two men? They were gorgeous and hot and amazing in bed. And she knew for a fact they had only shown her just a peek of what they could do.

"I say we ask her and get it over with," Mick said.

Adam opened his mouth to answer, but she decided it was better to face this head on.

"Just what is it that you want to ask me?"

twelve

Adam glanced over at Serenity and sighed. She looked as if she had been well loved. Her hair was a rumbled mess of curls spilling over her shoulders. She had whisker burn on her neck. And, she was wearing one of his shirts. She was damned adorable even as she eyed them both suspiciously.

"Well?"

He looked at Mick and, of course, his lover had lost his ability to speak. Anytime there was a confrontation in a personal relationship, Mick wanted to smooth it over. If he couldn't, he shut down.

He turned back to Serenity.

"Why don't you have a seat and I'll get you something to drink," Adam suggested.

"Coffee, with cream."

He nodded and went about the task. She sat at the bar. He set the coffee mug in front of her.

"So?"

"Drink. If we are going to talk about this, I want you awake."

"If not, the discussion might just wake you up," Mick muttered. He was the one who pushed this so fast and now he was complaining? Typical Mick.

"Go ahead. Give me the sell," she said. She didn't look as wary now, but there was a guarded quality to her words. It was the false bravado that hit him. He had an idea that as a former child actor, Serenity knew just how to handle a situation like this.

"You know we've been together for a while."

She nodded.

"We also play."

She cocked her head and studied him for a long minute. Then, she straightened her head to take another sip.

"Play at what?"

He glanced at Mick again, who apparently was overly interested in what was in his coffee cup.

"When we are with women, we like to engage in bondage and submission."

She said nothing as she took another sip of coffee.

He glanced at Mick, who was now paying attention.

"And?" she asked.

"It's that...

Why was he having a hard time coming up with an explanation for her? Before, it had never been a problem. Lay it out on the line, and if the woman wasn't interested, no big deal. This time, it seemed more important. He had to word it just right, or he would scare her off.

"Yes? Wait, you expected me to be freaked out?"

He nodded. She burst out laughing.

"What's so funny?" Mick asked.

"Sorry. You two really didn't hear all the stories about my wild and crazy teenage years, did you?"

They both shook their heads.

"Amazing." She smiled. "Truly amazing, but it doesn't shock me. Remember, I brought that box over and it was from a very well-known supplier of BDSM toys. I had a feeling, although it was hard for me to think that either of you would be the sub."

Mick snorted.

"No. We aren't subs, although we tend to have one lead when it comes to the play."

"So, when you're with a woman you like to do that, but you didn't try last night. Not that I'm complaining, but why?"

"Why?"

"Yeah, you didn't try. With me."

Feeling more at ease now, he grabbed his coffee and sat on the stool next to hers.

"We would never spring that on you like that. If you have been in the life, then we wouldn't have a problem with it."

"So, responsible deviants? Oh, don't look like that, Mick. I'm joking. Remember, I grew up in Hollywood. I was one step away from being sold on the street."

"What?"

"What I mean is that my mother lived off me from the time I was five. It isn't that much different than selling your soul, only that you have a choice. And, as a child, I saw a lot of things I shouldn't have seen. No child should. Hell, most adults shouldn't. I am your typical hippy California chick. Live and let live. But, I don't know that much about BDSM or the rules. There are rules, right?"

"Yeah, but we," he said motioning among the three of them, "make up the rules."

She slanted him a look and her mouth curved. "I don't particularly like rules."

"Oh, I have a feeling she's challenging us," Mick said, excitement filling his voice.

"Hold on. I don't know enough about it, and I want to learn. So, are there good websites for me to look at?"

"How about a trip to Rough 'n Ready?" Adam asked.

"That's brilliant," Mick said.

"Uh, what's Rough 'n Ready?"

"A BDSM club in Honolulu," Adam said.

"And they have a satellite on the North Shore, but I prefer the original," Mick said. "I'm sure we can get a guest pass from Ross."

"Ross?" She rolled her eyes. "Geez, I sound like a parrot."

Adam smiled. "You have to learn Mick speak. When he gets excited, he jumps from topic to topic."

"Yeah, I've noticed."

"We can go tonight," Mick said. The moment he did, there was a flash of panic in her expression before she quickly hid it. Adam forgot that before becoming a photographer, she'd made a living at acting.

"Hey, slow down. We just sprung it on her. I think we need a little time to get used to this."

She gave him a grateful look. "It's intriguing but let me think about it. I'm still getting used to the idea that you two want to keep me around past last night."

He knew from the tone of her voice that she wasn't kidding. Adam rose from the stool, then spun her around to face him. Caging her in by placing his hands on the counter behind her, he leaned in and brushed his mouth over hers. Neither of them closed their eyes.

"Fuck," Mick said. "That's fucking sexy."

When Adam pulled back, he leaned over to Mick and kissed him.

"Now *that's* sexy," she said with a laugh.

They both turned to her and she didn't hesitate. Just as Adam had, she leaned forward and kissed Mick, sucking on his tongue before moving away.

"Be right back," Mick said as he made his way to the bedroom.

"Should we join him?" she asked.

Adam shook his head but said nothing else. Instead, he leaned forward and pulled her bottom lip into his mouth and sucked. She closed her eyes and shuddered.

"You two know exactly what to do to push my buttons."

He cocked his head to the side and studied her. "Other men didn't?"

"Maybe it's because it's both of you, sort of the yin and yang of it."

Mick returned with a couple of condom packages and tossed them on the counter. Adam stepped aside and let Mick take his place. Mick took her by the waist and picked her up, dropping her on the counter.

"I'm ready for a tasty morsel," Mick said. He squatted in front of her and without hesitation, he set his mouth on her pussy. Damn.

Serenity let loose a long, loud moan as she let her head fall back. Adam knew there were a few toys they could play with, even if she hadn't agreed to submit, yet. He went to the bedroom and opened the drawer where he knew Mick had put the toys. He'd washed them all in anticipation of getting her in bed. He grabbed the vibrator and headed back to the kitchen. When he returned, Mick had upped his game, adding a finger. Serenity was shivering, her need to come so easy to see.

Adam didn't say anything. He just turned on the vibrator. Mick pulled back and smiled at him.

"I like your thinking."

Adam stepped up and pressed the head of the vibrator against her clit. Mick continued to finger her, adding another finger.

"I want to see you come over and over."

She opened her mouth, her eyes still closed. Adam turned the speed up, pressed harder against her clit. She came apart. With a shout, she convulsed her orgasm sweeping through her.

"Oh, God," Adam said. The reverence in Mick's voice was easy to understand. She was fucking beautiful when she came. When she came down, he upped the speed once more and sent her hurdling over into another orgasm.

This time when she recovered, he moved the vibrator away from her pussy. She opened her eyes.

"You are responsive."

She shook her head. "Never have been before. Like I said, you both just know what buttons to push."

"Hmm," Mick said as he started to unbutton the shirt.

She removed it and set it on the counter behind her. Mick didn't hesitate. He leaned forward and took a nipple into his mouth. Adam joined him. It didn't take long before she was squirming again on the counter. He scraped his teeth over the tip and she gasped.

He pulled back and gave her nipple a pinch.

"Our girl likes a little pain with pleasure," he said to Mick.

"Well, why don't we go for pleasure for right now."

"I really don't like when you talk about me like that."

Adam turned to her. She was lying. It was a turn on.

"Really?" He pressed his hand against her pussy, slipping two fingers into her. "I think you like it a lot."

Mick hummed as he undid his jeans and slipped them off. He was hard, a drop of precum wetting the head of his cock. He bent over and slipped Adam's cock into his mouth for a couple of pumps. The sweet, salty taste of his cum danced over his taste buds.

"Oh, there is something else our girl likes," Mick said, gesturing with his head toward Serenity.

Her face flushed again. "Yeah, I liked that a lot."

"Duly noted, for later," Adam said as he moved away. He undressed as fast as he could, then he grabbed the condoms, tossing one to Mick.

"Wait," she said.

He offered her a smile. "Not at once, but just in case we both want to feel our tight, little pussy, best to be prepared."

Since he'd already had the honor, he let Mick take control. Mick pulled her to the edge of the counter. He entered her in one hard thrust. She gasped, then moaned as he started to move. He lifted her legs to his hips and started to fuck her harder.

Adam stepped closer and skimmed his hand down Mick's back to his ass. As he continued to thrust in and out of Serenity, Adam slipped a finger into Mick's ass.

"Oh, shit, yeah," Mick muttered. The sound of slapping skin filled the kitchen and after a while, Adam couldn't hold back.

Adam removed his finger and stepped up behind Mick. Mick stopped moving.

"Lay back, babe," Mick said. When Serenity did, he leaned over a little to give Adam a better position.

Adam settled his hands on Mick's hips, as he pressed his cock inside of his ass. When Adam was fully seated inside of him, Mick started to move again.

Together they worked a rhythm. Serenity moaned as they started to speed up.

"That's it, babe. I want you to come again. I want to feel all those muscles on my cock, pulling me deeper into your pussy."

Adam slowed down so he could peek over Mick's shoulder.

"Damn, she's pretty. Her gorgeous breasts just bouncing every time you thrust into her."

"Yeah," Mick said. "But this…"

He pressed his thumb against her clit and she came again, arching up against Mick. This time she screamed again.

"Oh, damn," he said as he increased the speed of his thrusts again. Mick and he continued, then Mick thrust into Serenity one more time, groaning. That sound pulled Adam's orgasm from him. It surprised him at the force of it. He shouted as he thrust harder and faster. He finally gave himself over to the pleasure.

When he recovered, he realized he had collapsed onto Mick, who had collapsed onto Serenity. She was holding the weight of two men. It took all his strength to push himself up and then pull out of Mick.

"Mick."

"Hmm," is all he said as he wrapped his mouth around one of Serenity's nipples.

"Hey, you're too heavy, get up."

With a sigh, he pushed himself up and gave Adam a dirty look.

"Oh, don't be mad. We need to shower," he said wiggling his eyebrows.

Mick smiled, then he picked up Serenity, who had been

dozing on the counter apparently. He lifted her up and over his shoulder.

"Wait, what?" she asked.

"Shower time," Mick said as he headed back to their room.

She lifted her head up and looked at Adam. "Shower time?"

"You'll love it, believe me."

He definitely wouldn't mind starting more days just as they had today.

thirteen

They gorged themselves on pancakes and Portuguese sausage later that morning. Serenity had never been one to shy away from food, but she hadn't eaten this much in a long time. Of course, she hadn't had hot monkey sex with two guys before either. If they kept at it this way, she would need to up her game. For that, she needed fuel.

"What are your plans for today?" Adam asked as he pushed his plate away.

"Not sure. I was thinking about doing a play day for shoots at the beach."

"A play day?"

She shrugged. "I work, but mostly I enjoy the fact that I live in Hawaii. Just veg out at the beach. Do you two have to work?"

Adam shook his head, but it was Mick who answered.

"We normally work only four days a week, unless we get a job that pays better."

"It's actually a great day for a ride," Adam said.

She had seen them go out on their Harleys once or twice, but it hadn't been that often. They had hit the rainy season.

"Yeah. Have you ever ridden around the island on a bike?" Mick asked.

She shook her head.

"Then we must do that," Mick said. "We could pick a beach and just go there for the day."

"Mick."

"What?"

Adam shook his head, but she didn't get the communication.

"Listen, if you two want to be alone, then just say so. Won't hurt my feelings."

But it did a little bit. She knew she was the new member of the relationship and needed to learn where she fit. The guys were the ones in a long-term relationship. She had no idea where the three of them were headed, and she needed to make sure to remember that.

"No." Adam sighed. "Not what I meant at all. I was trying to let Mick know not to pressure you."

"I'm not pressuring her. Do you feel pressured, Seri?"

She blinked at the use of a nickname. Only Nicola used that nickname for her.

"No. Not at all, and a ride around the island sounds fantastic." Mick smiled. "But, today, I want to do some shooting, and I need my equipment for that. I definitely want to do that in the future, though."

They didn't say anything, just kept staring at her.

"So, did you two want to make a day of it?"

Mick looked at Adam, who smiled. "Sounds like a fantastic idea."

"YOU NEED TO SLOW IT DOWN," ADAM SAID.

Mick looked at him. The man held him by the heart, but sometimes he drove Mick crazy. He liked to plan and plot. That was good a lot of the time, but sometimes jumping in was the better way.

"I'm not going too fast. Jesus Christ, Adam. We had a threesome with our neighbor last night. It's not like asking her to ride around the island today was pushing her over the edge."

He buttoned his pants and looked up at Mick. "I just don't want her to feel overwhelmed by us. I don't want to scare her off."

Mick snorted. "We asked her about engaging in a BDSM relationship this morning and she didn't even blink."

Adam didn't argue back, which was one of his favorite things to do.

"Hey, what's up?" Mick asked.

"You rush, and I want to take it slow."

"No. You think you want to take it slow, but you don't. What you want is me to push you."

"She's different."

Yeah, he knew it. They'd shared a handful of women, but none of them had been this emotionally connected. Mick had an idea that it would be different with her. It was the connection he'd made that first day when she had smiled at him. His heart had zinged. That hadn't happened since he met Adam.

"She is, but I have a feeling she is okay with telling us when to back off."

"Okay, but just remember, slow and steady."

Mick watched as he pulled his t-shirt on, and inwardly sighed as he watched all that delicious bronze flesh disappear beneath it. The man did have a set of pecs and abs he liked to explore. Mainly with his mouth.

"Hey, eyes up here, perv," Adam said, but Mick heard the laughter in his voice.

"I promise, no pressure." He slipped his arms around Adam's waist. "But no dragging your feet. I don't want to miss this opportunity."

"Okay."

But he could tell from his tone that Adam wasn't convinced of his plan. He knew it would work. They just needed to let her taste how good it could be with them. She wouldn't be able to resist the idea.

THEY TOOK THE JEEP OUT FOR THE RIDE. IT WAS one of those spectacular days that had drawn both he and Mick to Hawaii in the first place.

The sun was high in the sky and the air was sweet from the morning rain. It was hard to remember their life in the military. One shit assignment after another, dealing with the worst scum in the world.

This was infinitely better.

"What are you thinking?" Serenity asked him.

He glanced over at her. He was driving and she was in the passenger seat beside him. She'd pulled her hair up into a messy bun, and she had sunglasses on, so he couldn't see her expression. But her voice was just inquisitive.

"That living here is better than hanging out in the desert hunting terrorists."

"A-fucking-men," Mick said from the backseat.

She chuckled. It was low and throaty, the one that always made his blood stir.

"I can understand that. When I left LA, I went to Washington state for a year."

"Seattle?"

She shook her head. "Forks. I wanted a change from Southern Cali."

"That is definitely a change," Adam said.

She nodded. "It rained all the time and, at first, it was wonderful. I would go out in it and dance around. Then, not so much."

"So, where did you go after that?" Mick asked.

If Adam hadn't glanced over at her, he wouldn't have seen the way her mouth tightened. But she answered.

"Arizona for a while. Then Colorado. After that, here. Actually, I came here for a vacation, not my first. But it was the first time I wasn't spending my time hiding from the paparazzi. This time, I rented a little cottage on the North Shore. And that's when it happened."

"What?" Adam asked, although he noted to ask her about the paparazzi comment later.

"That click. Like something just seemed right being here. I moved over here two months later."

"Just like that?"

She nodded. "And I have no desire to move away."

The light changed and he pushed aside the need to ask more questions. He wanted to know everything. What had caused her to walk away from her life, what horrors did she deal with? He knew they were lurking there behind the happy smile. He didn't think she was hiding anything from them, or that she was unstable. Far from it. It seemed that she had battled her demons and walked away victorious.

Of course, no one walked away without scars. That kind of stuff lurked. There were quiet moments that something would pass over her expression. He knew it wasn't his right to ask. Not yet. Doing so would probably have her shutting them out, which was not acceptable.

That thought gave him pause. Just like Mick had said, the only other lover he had felt so possessive of had been Mick. Until now.

"Do you mind going out to Ko' Olina?" She asked, breaking into his thoughts. "I want to get some pics of the tidal pools."

"Sure," he said.

She gave him that sunny smile and just like when she chuckled, his blood sang. He needed to be the strong one to make sure they didn't rush her. Mick would always be full steam ahead, but Adam had to ensure they did this right.

"And we can eat over there," Mick said.

"Good lord. You need to eat again?" she asked.

"I'm always hungry for all kinds of things."

Adam still couldn't see her eyes, but he had an idea she rolled her eyes.

She leaned closer to Adam. "How do you put up with him?"

"I'm just using him for sex."

She threw back her head and laughed. The glorious sound danced on the air around him. And for right now, that was enough.

fourteen

A week after their first night together, Adam drove over to Jillian and Conner's. Mick had a job and Serenity had some kind of meeting with a vendor in Honolulu. He wasn't sure about what, but it sounded like someone wanted to sell her pictures, to tourists of course. A huge number of photographers made money that way, but from what Serenity had said, she did better than most. So, he decided to head on over to their old stomping grounds.

Adam watched Jillian as she watched her son play in the sand. She was leaning back against her beach chair, sunglasses on, a big straw hat, and wearing a white sundress. Her hand rested on her massive pregnant belly. Every now and then she would rub it.

"I hate this weather."

He chuckled. "You hate everything right now."

She gave him a dirty look, then turned her attention to

the waves. It was the slow time of year and since the rain the other night, it had turned unbearably humid. He could understand that she was uncomfortable.

"So, you're going with my husband over to Maui. Any shenanigans planned?"

He snorted. "Like that man will do anything without you knowing. And, it's a short trip."

She sniffed in annoyance. It didn't matter what he said. He always annoyed her these days. It was like this last time, so he was ready for it.

"Why are you out here bugging me and not having fun with Serenity?"

It didn't surprise him that Jillian had picked up on their relationship. It wasn't like they tried to hide it from her, but she hadn't seen the three of them together. They had been lost in their own little world, just the three of them. It seemed that they had an unspoken agreement to keep it to themselves for right now. It wasn't that they were ashamed. Right now, he had a feeling they all wanted to keep their relationship safe, guarded. Each of them were trying to figure out where things were going. Pressure from people outside of the threesome would put more stress on them.

He glanced out at the waves and then back to Jillian. Her gaze had moved back to her son. Her observance came from two different areas. One, their friendship. Two, it was the writer in her. Many people didn't realize how much she observed in their behavior. Especially when it came to romance.

"She had a meeting in Honolulu with a vendor. Plus, she's busy working on a book."

"She's writing?"

He shook his head and looked out at a surfer on the waves. It was still surreal that he lived in Hawaii. As humid as it was paradise. They had their issues but it was still beautiful every day. And now, things seemed settled...almost like they were completed with Serenity in their lives.

"Earth to Adam."

He glanced at her again, then back out at the surfer. "What?"

"The book?"

"Oh, no. It's a picture book of Hawaii, but not like those kinds of touristy books. There will be a lot of pretty pics, but she wants to show all the sides of Hawaii."

She said nothing and he looked at her. The look on her face worried him. She looked like she was going to cry.

"What?"

She sighed. "You're in love with her."

He felt a sharp punch to the gut. "No."

"If not, you're falling."

"I haven't known her long enough for that."

"There's a set time limit before you can fall in love?"

He heard the sarcasm in her voice, and he knew if he continued denying it, he would make an ass out of himself. That wasn't enough to stop him.

"Stop that. We have no idea where this is going."

She tsked. "I thought for sure that Mick would be the first one to fall. But maybe..."

"What?"

She laughed. "Oh, someone is so testy when he's in love."

Dammit. "Stop that."

"If you promise me one thing."

He nodded. Anything to get her to quit talking about love and Serenity.

"What?"

"Give it a chance."

"Give what a chance?"

"Falling in love." He opened his mouth to argue with her, but she stopped him. "I know you love Mick, but I have a feeling you fought that too. Now there is this woman. She's new to both of you, but I sense it. Something has shifted in your universe. Just don't freak out like you do when things change."

"I don't freak out."

She slipped her glasses down her nose and stared over them at him.

"Really? You threw a fit when Mick's parents sold their house."

That was true. But it had been his first real home, the one place he had been accepted. It was irrational and stupid, but he couldn't seem to keep himself from freaking out, a little.

"Why don't you help me up, then go spend some time with Serenity."

He opened his mouth to say that Mick wasn't going to be there, but she stopped him.

"You want Mick there because he's your safe space, but also because he can help you keep her at arm's length. When it is just the two of you, it might be too hard for you to fight."

He hated that she was right, but again, fighting her would just make it worse.

"Remember what I said. Go spend some time with her. You don't know each other well and maybe that will ease your worries."

"First, I have no worries, and second, how much better can I know her...if you get my drift?"

"Sexually, yes. But now, you need to get to know *her*. I bet you barely know anything about her childhood, or her life after she left acting."

Her being right was not good for him. But then, it wasn't like he was avoiding it.

"What?" she asked.

He shrugged. "Seriously, I meant to ask her questions."

"But?"

Adam shoved his hand through his hair. "Okay, I lose control. I see her and all I can think about is getting her naked."

There was a long moment of silence, then she laughed in his face.

"Gee, thanks for being so understanding," he said.

"Oh, my, how the mighty have fallen. Mr. Big Bad Dom can't control himself. This is too much. And, more than likely, Mick is the same way with her, right?"

He nodded.

She shook her head. "You're both head over heels for her. How about Serenity?"

He wanted to deny her assumption, but it would be stupid and false. He was falling for her. "It's only been a week since our first time together."

"So?"

"It's too soon."

He couldn't see her eyes behind her mirrored sunglasses, but he had a feeling she rolled her eyes.

"It's not. Don't push it, but don't short yourselves either. If this is something you want, make sure that she knows."

"Oh, she knows."

"I don't mean sex. I mean HEA."

"What?"

"All these years I've talked about writing my books and you haven't paid attention? HEA equals happily ever after."

He grunted. He wasn't ready to admit out loud that was what he wanted. He wanted the three of them together. Mick had no problem admitting it, but he had always been the dreamer. Adam needed his feet firmly fixed on the ground.

Until Serenity.

She had changed the dynamics of Mick and Adam's relationship. He had known she would, but it was a bigger change than he had expected.

"Does she play?"

Both Jillian and her husband Conner lived in the life.

"No, but she is interested."

"It's not like it is something that you need though, right?"

He nodded. "But, I think she's definitely a submissive. She likes to do things we tell her, and she is okay with both of us controlling things. Mick wants to take her to Rough 'n Ready."

"That is a good idea." Jillian slapped him on the shoulder. "Come on. Quit thinking too much and help me up."

He stood, then held his hand out for her. She took it and he helped her up. She cringed.

"Are you okay?" he asked, embarrassed that his voice had risen in alarm.

She smiled. "No, other than being a fat pregnant woman."

"I'll get Sammy."

"I am okay with that. I'll start walking back up to the house."

"Let me help you."

"You can't leave Sammy."

"I'll have my eye on him. You can't walk up there by yourself."

He took her by the hand, and while keeping his eye on the little boy, he helped her up the incline. Once they reached the top, he let her go.

"I'll be right back."

"Okay. And Adam?"

He turned around. "Yeah."

"Remember to be happy."

For a moment, he didn't catch her drift, but when he did, he nodded.

"No, really, you three deserve it."

The way she phrased that was weird, but he only nodded and started back down the incline. Jillian was right about one thing. He needed to know more about the woman he and Mick were falling in love with. The best way to do that was spend time with her. With that in mind, he set off to gather Sammy and his toys, so he could head back to his house and Serenity.

fifteen

S erenity had just closed her email and stepped away from her computer when she heard the vibrations of Adam's Harley. He had gone out a couple hours earlier without stopping by. It didn't bother her...much. Okay, it bothered her a lot, but she couldn't say anything to him about it. They had no set rules to their relationship, right? They were just having fun, and that was what she liked.

Only, now, it made her feel sad that he hadn't stopped by.

Trying her best not to look out the window and make him think she was a creeper, she thought about a nap. She was low on sleep and wanted to do some more night time shoots. Before she could make it to her room, she heard footsteps on her lanai, then a knock.

She hesitated.

"Serenity."

Damn, he knew she was home. And why was she being such an idiot by not going to the door?

She walked over and opened it. He was leaning against the doorjamb, a sleeveless t-shirt showing off his biceps and old jeans that rode low on his hips.

"You didn't have to work today?"

He shook his head and then let his gaze slip down her body. Dammit, when he did that, it made her feel as if he were touching her.

sixteen

A few days later, Serenity found herself alone. The guys had a job together on Maui, and she was taking the time to work on her book. Unfortunately, she was spending more time thinking about the guys rather than doing her work.

These two men were starting to get to her. She knew that they probably did this all the time, but it was new for her. Hell, she'd only had two normal relationships in her lifetime, only one as an adult. James had been her first love, a costar, and just as screwed up as she was. They remained in touch via email.

She met Brad about a year after she moved to Forks. He was funny and sweet. He'd soothed her soul and never asked her for more than she could give. In the end, both acknowledged that they wanted other things and parted as friends. It was part of the reason she had moved to Arizona. She needed a change and nothing says change like moving from Forks to

Tucson. Since then, she'd had a few hookups here and there, but nothing too serious. She wasn't built for that.

Her relationship with Brad had taught her that. He had been willing to wait, to work with her on building a long-lasting relationship. She hadn't wanted to even try. He had been perfect for her, but she couldn't tell him she wanted him around forever.

She shook herself out of her funk and rose to get some more coffee. It was odd that she hadn't slept well at all last night. In less than two weeks, Adam and Mick had become such a huge part of her life that she couldn't sleep without them in bed with her.

She'd just finished doctoring her coffee when she heard a car drive up.

Jillian.

She walked to the front door and watched as the mother to be pulled herself out of her car. She looked even bigger than before.

"Hey," she said, a sunny smile curving her lips. "Sorry for just popping in."

But nothing in her expression or tone of voice told Serenity that she actually felt that way. As she waddled her way over to the front steps, Serenity studied her. Was she there to tell her to back off?

"Good lord, I think I might just burst if I don't have this child soon. I feel like a beached whale."

Serenity shook her head as she held the door open for Jillian. "You look beautiful."

"That's sweet. Did Conner pay you to say that?"

She chuckled. "No. And you are. You know you are one of those women other pregnant women look at with hatred."

"Oh. That's sweet."

"Sit."

Jillian did as instructed, as a smile played about her lips.

"Is that coffee?"

Serenity nodded. "Want some?"

"Want, yes. But I can't have any."

"Oh, sorry."

"No worries. I can at least enjoy the smell." Then silence descended.

"Is there a particular reason for this visit?"

"I needed to get out of the house. I'm on hiatus from writing and it is about to drive me insane. This is my last voyage out for a while. Once Conner gets back, I will be on lockdown unless I go out with him."

"I can imagine."

"Usually I would bother Adam and Mick, but since they moved, I can't do that. So, I came over here."

And there it was. She knew there was a reason Jillian had come over, and it had nothing to do with being restless. She had come to warn her off.

"Out with it, Jillian."

Jillian blinked, then another smile curved her lips. "I like smart women. And you are definitely smart."

"Are you here about the guys?"

"In a way."

"I appreciate that you feel the need to protect them, but I can assure you..."

Her voice trailed off when Jillian laughed out loud. "What?"

"Oh," she said between chuckles. "You almost made me wet my pants with that laugh."

Annoyance and something close to fear curled in her gut.

"So, if not that, what?"

Jillian sighed. "Now, I have made you angry. I'm sorry. I didn't mean that. Part of it is needing to have someone else to talk to. As I said, without the guys there, I have no one to bug."

"And there's no one else?"

She shrugged. "I like my space. I'm sure you understand."

It was true, having her own space was very important.

"And you know it's hard to make friends when you work from home. A solitary job leads to a less than healthy friend list. Conner is on Maui with the guys until tonight."

"Should you be left alone?"

She snorted. "I can handle anything that comes up. Plus, I do have friends, but many of them have jobs."

"Ah, yes. Hard to find someone who can just take off for an afternoon and go running around."

"My best friend, Conner's sister, lives in Miami. A huge percentage of my friends work at Rough 'n Ready."

"Ah, and so not much time if you're exhausted at the end of the day. Different schedule and all that."

"Exactly. See, you get it. I'm getting on Conner's nerves. No writing, stuck at home. He is not used to a dependent wife."

"Should have thought about that before he got you pregnant a second time."

"I knew I was going to like you when I met you."

Silence descended again.

"And the other thing?"

"What?"

"The other thing you were talking about. You said that it was one reason."

"I just wanted to check you out more."

"That's better. I deal better with up front questions."

"Then we should get along just fine."

"You're worried about Mick and Adam. I guess they told you we were involved."

"Yes, but I wanted to make sure you were okay."

She blinked. It had been so long since anyone had worried about her. At least, not unless she was involved with the person.

"I'm fine."

She paused when taking a sip of water and set the glass down. She leaned forward, causing some of her braids to slip over her shoulders.

"Are you sure? And I'm not asking because I think you are weak. I try not to mettle, but the guys are sometimes... obtuse."

"They've been really sweet."

"Please tell me that's not all they've been."

Even after all her years in Hollywood, she had been sheltered. She knew about things, but people rarely asked her about her sex life. Friends wouldn't. Strangers never had a problem with it.

"Good," Jillian said. "Just so you know, they are going to be looking for more than just a good time."

Yes, she had sensed that too. Serenity had no idea how to feel about a long-term relationship with one man, let alone two. Serenity knew she was not built for that kind of life anymore.

"I don't know if I'll be ready for a relationship with them or not. One thing I do know is that I will try my best not to hurt them."

"Oh, honey I'm not worried about them," Jillian said. "They've never taken this chance before, but I think both know what they want. My main worry is that they're going to rush you and you're going to freak out and push them away."

"So, you're not worried that I might hurt them?"

Jillian shrugged and leaned back in the chair. "Being hurt, it's part of being in love. You can't have one without the other, just the way it goes."

Serenity wished she could be so laid back about falling for them. Knowing that pain came with the relationship and that it was worth it. But, they had her head and her heart twisted around.

"I can see that you have a lot of craziness going on in that head of yours."

She focused on Jillian, who offered her an understanding smile.

"How do you know that?"

"I've been there myself. One man is hard enough to deal

with, but two would make me insane. You have a lot to deal with, Serenity."

"Yeah."

"And I know it isn't easy. My best friend has a relationship with two men."

"Conner's sister?"

She nodded. "He wasn't exactly happy about it, especially since both work for the company. But, once he saw how they felt about her, it was enough to convince him. Well, mostly. Every now and then he gets a little grumpy about it."

"I can't even think about siblings. Sometimes I thought I would want one. It wasn't easy being an only child. Now, though, as an adult, I'm not sure I'd like the idea that he or she might feel the need to pass judgement on my choices."

"Weird, right? I don't have any either, but Conner is a bit older than his sister. He helped raise her after their parents died, so he is somewhat more protective."

She rubbed her hand over her stomach and Serenity followed the motion. "Oh, God, this Demon Seed is going to kill me. Kick, kick, kick." She smiled at Serenity. "Want to feel?"

Her first response danced on the tip of her tongue. *No.* Not because she didn't want to, but she had decided a long time ago not to have children. She just wasn't built for it. But...

She reached her hand out and placed it on Jillian's tummy. It only took a second before she felt the kick.

"Oh, wow."

"Yeah, so I haven't slept through the night in a long time."

Just that simple touch did exactly what she didn't want. The longing to have a child had been something she had fought for years, but now that she had started this relationship with Mick and Adam, her mind kept straying to the idea of a little one.

"Hey, Earth to Serenity."

She blinked and focused on Jillian once more.

"Sorry."

"No worries. You just looked sad there for a moment."

"Just an odd thought."

Jillian looked like she wanted to say more but she refrained. Thankful, Serenity stood.

"I have some mac bread I made up. You want some?"

"God, yes. I didn't like sweet stuff up until last week. All of a sudden, I feel a need to suck down sugar by the pound."

As she went about the task of cutting the bread, she decided to push the thoughts of babies or long-term relationships out the window. Going down that road was going to lead to heartache. Hell, both had it written all over them. But thinking about a tiny little person with curly blond hair, or a dark-haired baby with striking blue eyes would depress her. She could deal with a death of a relationship. The death of a dream was something different and she'd had that happen in her life already.

"Here you go," she said, handing the bread to Jillian.

She took it with a smile, but it faded when she saw Serenity's expression.

"What's wrong?"

She shook her head.

"No," Jillian said. "Tell me."

"I just don't want to think about certain things."

"Certain things like a future with the guys?"

She shrugged and sat down again. "I learned a long time ago that hoping for things don't make them come true."

Jillian sat back and stared at her. "Just remember that sometimes things work out. That maybe, just maybe, the guys are exactly what you need."

She wanted to argue, but Jillian's determined look kept her from saying anything. She was close to tears and she didn't know why. If she had to argue with the other woman, she might start sobbing.

"You're right. Do you want anything to drink with that?"

"Water would be great."

She went to get the water for Jillian and pushed her worries aside. There was nothing to be done about it anyway. She'd enjoy the moment with these two men and worry about tomorrow, tomorrow.

SEVENTEEN

Mick grabbed his overnight backpack and followed Adam and Conner out the door of the private jet. It had been a long four days in Maui, but both he and Adam had made a good amount of money. One more week on another job in Kauai, and they would have enough money saved up for a vacation.

"It seems like we've been gone for weeks," Adam said.

Mick nodded, knowing exactly what he had been talking about. They'd always had each other, and while they often took separate jobs, having someone waiting for them at home made a difference. Just knowing that Serenity was there waiting for them had his libido humming. It also warmed his heart. She had added a dimension to their relationship that had taken them by surprise.

"Next week you're going with Jake," Conner said as they approached their vehicles. "I'm staying close to home for the next few weeks."

"Yeah. I wouldn't want to deal with Jillian going into labor and you being on another island. Somehow, I think we might get blamed for it."

Conner chuckled. "More than likely. See y'all later."

"Sure thing."

Mick climbed into the passenger seat as Adam started up the SUV.

They drove out of the airport up onto H-1 in the direction of Pali Highway.

"I am so fucking tired," Adam said.

"Yeah. We might be getting too old for this."

He smiled as he sped around a pokey sedan. "Why don't you call Serenity and let her know we're back on the island?"

He said nothing for a moment, which gained him a side glance from Mick. "What?"

"Nothing."

"No. That silence meant something, especially coming from you. You are never quiet."

"Fuck off," he said with little heat. "I'm just happy you seem to be accepting Serenity."

"I never said I didn't accept her. I just worry that everything happened so fast, that she might get overwhelmed."

He nodded as he called her. She answered on the second ring.

"Hey," she said, her voice husky with sleep. "Whatcha doing?"

"We just landed. Adam wanted me to let you know."

"Okay."

"You were sleeping?"

"Yeah. No. I'm not sure."

He chuckled. "Go back to sleep."

"'kay. Love you guys."

Then she hung up the phone. Adam took the Pali Highway exit and still, Mick hadn't hung up the phone.

"What?" he asked.

"Nothing, just she was sleepy. Never mind."

"No, something happened."

Mick hesitated, thinking about the words again. "She told me she loved us."

Adam blinked. "Loved us?"

"Yes, she said, 'love you guys,' then she hung up."

A car horn sounded behind them, so Adam snapped out of it and turned onto the highway.

"She was asleep when you called?"

"I think so. If not, pretty dammed close."

"Uh."

"Yeah."

At first, there were no feelings at all. He was stunned. She hadn't given him any inkling that she had those feelings. Sure, there was that connection in bed, but she hadn't said a word about it.

"What's wrong?" Adam asked.

"It's kind of fast."

"Really? You're worried about this going too fast? Are you kidding me?"

Joy danced around the edges of his heart, but there was also worry. Did she really love them or was she just half asleep and not knowing any better? Or maybe, she was confusing lust with love.

"It figures you're having second thoughts."

"And you don't?"

He shrugged. "Not really. I told you. There was this connection with her. We both said we felt it."

But did they feel it because it was real, or was it because they wanted to feel it? That she made them feel so good because together they made a good threesome?

"Hey, babe, stop worrying."

He glanced at Adam. "That's usually my line."

"Truth is, you're worrying because this is real. Before it was always just for fun, but now things are real. We aren't just hooking up for a good time."

"I guess so."

"I know so. Stop worrying. That's usually my job."

He chuckled. "Yeah I guess so."

"And don't let it mess up tonight. I know both of us have been hankering for her."

That much was true. They'd been so tired on the job that they had fallen into bed together and not done much of anything else. Still, without her there, it felt like something was missing. That had never happened before.

"I guess so. But she was sleeping."

"Like we would let that stop us. I can't wait to sink inside of her."

Just hearing Adam put his own thoughts into words had his cock twitching. They'd made love every night they were gone, but as he had thought before, there had been something missing. Even when they were just sleeping, he knew both he and Adam had missed having Serenity in bed with them.

"Okay, I'll stop worrying, at least for tonight."

It was so late that it only took them another twenty minutes to make it back to the house. Adam parked the SUV in front of their house. Mick slipped out of the vehicle, then grabbed his overnight bag out of the backseat. He started to follow Adam up the steps to the house, but stopped.

It didn't feel right. And that was what had been freaking him out. Being in their house together, in this one and the ones they had lived in before this one had been one of the comforting feelings Mick had had. Now, it wasn't the same if Serenity wasn't there.

That one thought should have freaked him out a little. He liked to jump before thinking. It had worked for him in the past. Ignoring all those warnings, he made an easy decision.

"Hey, take this," he said waiting for Adam to turn around before he tossed the bag toward him.

He turned on his heel and strode to her house. When he reached her front door, it was locked, of course. He knocked on it. Something crashed to the floor and then he heard a very grumpy Serenity cussing.

She opened the door. Her hair was a mess of curls on top of her head and she was wearing an old tank top with lettering so faded he couldn't read it. It skimmed her thighs, and he noticed she was only wearing panties with it.

"What?"

She didn't look like a woman who was welcoming one of her lovers home.

And in that instant, he knew he loved her. It had really crept up on him. Mick felt almost blindsided with the revelation.

"So, you just decided to knock on my door and stand there like an imbecile?"

That grumpy voice, along with her appearance, made it impossible to hold back. He grabbed her, then cupped her face with his hands. He couldn't say the words, not yet. So, he dipped his head down and kissed her. Even irritated with him, she didn't hesitate. Opening her mouth to him, she wrapped her arms around his neck. Slipping his hands down her body, he lifted her against him. Again, no hesitation. She wrapped her legs around his waist.

The kiss was sexual, but it was also so much more. He poured his feelings into it, letting her know without words what he felt. He wanted her. In their bed, and in their lives.

When he finally pulled back, they were both breathing heavily.

"Come home with us."

She peeked over his shoulder and he knew without looking that Adam was here. Then, she met his gaze again and gave him a small smile. "Of course."

Adam grabbed her keys and phone, locked the door to her house, and followed Mick as he carried her back to their house.

He set her on the bed, then shed his clothes. Adam

joined them. There was no play, no real plan. It seemed as if Adam could read his mind. This was about Serenity.

They stripped her of her clothes. Mick kissed his way down her body and settled between her legs. She was wet, ready for them to take her. It was amazing that just that little bit of foreplay--if anyone would call it that--could get her so aroused.

He set his mouth on her pussy, sliding his tongue along her dripping slit before he stole inside for a taste.

Fuck. Fuck. So damned perfect.

She moaned as he continued to lick her. Adam moved to her breasts, taking one nipple in his mouth as he pinched and teased the other. Mick lifted his head for a minute as he watched his lovers. Heat seared through his veins. As he continued to watch them, he slipped a finger into her damp passage.

"Oh, God," she murmured as she bowed up off the bed.

Adam moved on to her other breast, sucking it hard into his mouth. As he did that, Mick kept his gaze on the two of them while he lowered his head. He added another finger, then used his tongue to tease her clit. She shivered in reaction.

Mick watched Adam again. That arousal, that need struck him hard. This wasn't the typical lust Adam had for a woman they brought to bed. He was in love with Serenity also.

"Let me have a taste," Adam said, as he leaned down to kiss Mick.

Adam hummed as he drew Mick's tongue into his mouth.

He pulled back. "So fucking good."

Then they both set on her pussy once again. Mick pulled his fingers out of her, allowing Adam to lean down and slip his tongue between her pink lips.

Mick watched for a moment, relishing the image of Adam's dark head between her white thighs.

He looked up at Serenity, who was lost in the moment, her eyes closed, her moans growing louder by the moment. He knew from experience, she was close. He wanted to hear that, to watch it, but he also wanted to feel it.

"Hey, Adam."

Adam gave her one long last lick before he pulled back. Again, he kissed Mick, then sat up. He grabbed a couple of condoms, tossing one to Mick. Adam took the lube and covered his finger with it. Mick laid on the bed, then drew her over him. He didn't hesitate. He thrust into her to the hilt. She groaned and arched her back.

"Do you think you can take both of us?"

"Yessss," she said.

Adam slipped a finger between her cheeks, then he slowly entered her.

"Goddamnit," Adam said. "She's fucking good."

"Are you okay?" he asked her when they were both fully seated inside of her.

Together they started to move.

They had done this hundreds of times before with

different women, but this was special. She was special. It didn't take long before all of them were approaching their orgasms. Serenity came first, shaking and screaming both their names as she did.

They doubled their efforts now, both thrusting into her over and over again. She was barely done with her first orgasm, when her second one hit. She convulsed, her pussy clenching around him, pulling him deeper inside of her.

He lost it then, groaning as he thrust into her one more time as his orgasm slammed through him. He heard Adam do the same, his hoarse shout louder than his own.

Long moments later, they were still entangled together. Mick stirred, knowing they needed to check on Serenity. This was her first time with the two of them like this.

"Adam."

He stirred and lifted his head up. "What?"

"Serenity," he said.

Adam understood and moved. Serenity groaned.

"Hey," Mick said, brushing the hair off her face. "Are you okay?"

"Yeah, just a little sore."

He heard the water start in the bathroom. "Adam's starting a bath. You need a soak."

She nodded and mumbled against his shoulder. Adam returned and helped her up, then picked her up. Mick slipped out of bed and followed him to the bathroom.

"I can walk," she mumbled.

"Yeah, we know," Adam said.

Mick smiled. This was what he needed. Adam, Serenity, and him. Every worry Mick had had faded away when he realized there was no place else on earth he would rather be. And for right now, that worked for him.

eighteen

The next morning, Adam woke up to find himself tangled in the sheets with Serenity. He closed his eyes and tightened his grip on her. The scent of plumeria and the unique scent of Serenity. He opened his eyes again, he looked down at her. She slept like the dead as usual. He wanted nothing more than to slip into her again, but they had made love to her twice the night before. She needed her rest.

As carefully as he could, he slipped out of bed. After a quick trip to the bathroom, he slipped on a pair of board shorts and padded barefoot into the kitchen. The coffee had been brewed and one glance told him Mick was sitting on the back lanai. He filled a coffee cup up to the brim, took a sip, then headed out to sit with Mick. The sun was just peeking out over the horizon.

"Best view of the sunrise we've ever had."

Adam nodded as he took the seat next to Mick's.

"Looks like we might have some high winds tonight."

Which meant there was a chance that they could end up with power outages.

"Good thing we aren't planning on going anywhere," Adam said.

"And thank God we got that generator."

They sat in silence for a few moments watching the orange hues dance over the sky as the sun rose. Adam's mind went back to the night before. There had been something going on with Mick.

"So, you want to tell me about last night?"

Mick glanced at him, then back out over the beach to the water.

"What are you talking about?"

"You seemed a little possessed last night."

"Complaining?"

"Not one bit. But it wasn't just about sex last night."

For a long moment, he said nothing. He took a long sip of coffee. It was so unlike him that worry started to grow.

"Mick?"

"I just realized that I was in love with her last night."

Adam blinked. "You *just* realized that?"

Mick looked at him. "Yeah. What, you knew before I did?"

Adam chuckled. "Listen, you have always been obtuse but never to that extent."

"I didn't expect it to change so much."

The annoyance in Mick's voice almost made Adam smile. "What the hell are you talking about?"

Again, hesitation. "It's not just us. It's been us for so long, and I thought that was what I wanted."

"I thought that was your plan all along. You wanted a permanent woman in our bed."

"I didn't plan for this, okay?" He got up and started to pace. "I didn't expect that I wouldn't just want you in bed with me. It was like we were missing a part of ourselves when we were on the job. She wasn't there and while we were together, it wasn't the same."

Adam smiled and leaned back in his chair. "So, you realize now that this is a big deal. You didn't before."

"I did. It's just that, I didn't think she would matter so fucking much in just a few weeks. I can't even think of what it was like before her. I don't want to."

"And that's why I didn't want to do it in the beginning."

Mick stopped his pacing. "What?"

"I knew it would change everything. Good and bad. I also knew there was a chance that all of us could end up hurt in the end. Long term threesomes are not always easy to deal with."

Mick shoved both of his hands through his blond hair. It was nice to see him so frustrated. Ninety percent of the time, Adam was the one who suffered. He often found himself at odds with everything his lover wanted to do. Every now and then, Mick had to deal with the situation, and it was gratifying that Adam got a chance to witness it.

"So, what do we do?"

"What do you mean? Because you're feeling vulnerable you're worried?"

"I..." he fell silent.

"Exactly. Think of it from her perspective. We've had a relationship for years. She's the one taking the chance."

A noise sounded behind him and he turned to find Serenity watching them through the screen door. She was wearing one of their white dress shirts and probably nothing else. Her hair was a tangle of curls over her shoulders.

"Sorry, I didn't mean to eavesdrop, but you two were being so loud."

One glance in Mick's direction told Adam he wasn't ready to cover for them. So, he turned back to Serenity with a smile.

"No worries, love. You were the topic of discussion."

She blinked. "That's honest."

"Why lie? You heard us. Get a cup of coffee and join us."

She held up her hand to show she already had one. He motioned with his head.

She joined them, but she didn't hurry. When she reached them on the lanai, she stood apart from them. Adam didn't like that. If they were going to move on to a more established relationship, they were one unit. Not just them and her.

He stood, grabbed her hand, pulling her closer to him. Sitting back down, he said, "Sit down."

She moved to the other seat that Mick had just vacated. They needed another seat.

"No, over here." He patted his lap, then smiled up at her. Part of her stiffness seemed to dissolve, then she did as he requested.

"I don't know what you heard. We haven't done this before so we're bound to fuck things up. We're men."

She sighed and raised her gaze to his. "I thought you said you had."

"We played with women in threesomes. We never invited any of them into our lives."

She glanced at Mick, who was still standing off to the side. "I...I'm not coming in between you?"

He shook his head as he skimmed his hand over her thigh, moving the bottom edge of the shirt up.

"Not at all. It is just new and different. And because we're men, like I said, we fuck things up. See, Mick just realized he was in love with you."

Her eyes widened as she looked over at Mick. He glanced over to find his lover looking out over the ocean again. Idiot.

When she looked back at him, there were tears in her eyes.

"That makes you sad?"

She shook her head. "I only have one friend in the world I know loves me for me. She never put a price on our friendship. It was a new thing for me. Now this."

That was about the saddest thing in the world he'd ever heard. He had looked her up, saw that she had won a few awards, been nominated for a lot of fan favorite kind of things, and no one had ever said they loved her.

"What about your parents?"

"My parents were divorced and my mother...well, she saw me as a commodity. It was never that she just loved me for me. She loved me for what I could give her."

He sensed that Mick was paying attention now.

"Well, then this is a first for you too."

"What?"

"You have two men who are in love with you. In fact, I don't think either of us wants to think about being without you in our lives."

She blinked again, causing her tears to cascade down her cheeks.

"I'm sorry," Mick said rushing forward.

She shook her head. "Don't be. It makes me so happy."

"Yeah?" Mick asked.

She nodded and sniffed. "I think I might be in love with you two, also."

"You think?" Mick asked.

She shrugged. "I've never been in love before, so I guess this might be it. I feel happy most of the time, but also overwhelmed and scared." She closed her eyes and shook her head. "I sound like an idiot."

The next moment, Mick was kneeling beside them. He wrapped his arms around her.

"No. It's normal and probably amplified because you're dealing with two of us." Mick pulled back and then cupped her face. "I love you, Serenity."

Then he kissed her, long and deep. When he pulled back, Adam did the same.

"I love you, too."

She sighed and opened her mouth. "No. You take your time."

"Okay." She scrubbed her face dry. "I'm hungry."

Adam laughed. "Yeah, well so am I. I thought maybe we could go to Koko Head Café, after."

"After what?"

Mick was already moving into the house.

"After I have a little taste of Serenity."

He offered her a hand and she smiled. It was all he needed right now.

"Hmm, and I think I need a little taste of Mick and Adam."

He laughed as he led her back into the house.

nineteen

Serenity found herself alone on Monday morning. The guys had a job that would keep them off the island overnight. They had tried to talk her into going with them, but she had refrained. It wasn't as though she didn't want to go. In fact, it had taken all of her control not to jump at the chance.

She knew they had both been disappointed with her decision. Hell, so had she, but there were so many reasons for not going. First, they were going to be working the entire time. While a lot of people would prefer to spend time in a big comfy bed and maybe go to the spa, it wasn't her thing. Second, she thought she needed a little separation from Mick and Adam.

She sat on her small lanai, a coffee cup in her hand, and drew in a deep breath. She needed this time to think about them...and about being with them. Never in her life would she have thought she would be in a relationship with two men. One had always been a little too much for her, and now she had two men occupying her time.

What was it about them that drew her in? She couldn't put her finger on it. She had thought maybe it had to do with the fact that their personalities were so different. Mick was open and always looking for a good time. Adam liked to take his time and savor. Two sides to the same coin.

Before she could come up with a definitive answer, her phone rang. She saw her friend Nicola's face and wondered why she was calling her so early in the morning.

"Hey, what are you doing calling me?"

"Well, how nice. Did you get those manners at finishing school?" she asked, laughter filling her voice.

"Sorry. I, never mind. Kind of early for you."

"I'm not in the states. We're in Japan."

"Such a jet setter."

Nicola snorted. "Right. Anyway, I was calling because it looks like we are going to spend some time in Hawaii."

Happiness unfurled within her. It had been a long time since they had spent time in person together. "You are? And does this mean the very delicious Jensen Wulf will be accompanying you?"

"You can ask him yourself since you're on the speaker."

For a couple of seconds, Serenity said nothing. Her cheeks burned with embarrassment. Good God, had she really said that and had he heard? Then Nicola burst out laughing.

"Nicola Marie McCann."

"Sorry. Oh, God, I would have loved to see your face. It must have been priceless."

"Ha ha."

It took her another minute or two to calm down. "Yes, Jensen will be with me, so it should be a load of fun." A healthy dose of sarcasm filled her voice. "But, it looks like we'll be there for at least a month."

"That sounds great. When?"

"In a few weeks. We haven't secured the entire schedule, and I need to find a rental for us. We should get to spend a lot of time together."

"Great."

Serenity didn't have a lot of friends, but she counted Nicola as her best friend. They rarely got to spend any time together. A day here or there, but if Nicola was going to be there for a few weeks, they could really plan some girl days together.

"So, tell me what you've been up to? How's the picture book coming along?" Nicola asked.

"Going well. We had a big storm that I got some great shots of."

"And the neighbors?"

"What?"

"Last time we talked the new neighbors were moving in. Are they nice?"

"Hmm, yeah. Two men."

"Oh. Two men as in together or they are hetero?"

"Sort of both."

There was a long beat of silence.

167

"You talking in riddles makes me think you are trying to keep things from me."

Dammit.

Serenity hadn't contemplated having to explain the situation to friends and family. She had no family to speak of, but most of her friends were online. Nicola was different. She hadn't seen her in three years, but it almost seemed poetic that her former sober companion was planning a trip to Hawaii. Nothing had ever been easy with Nicola.

"They're bisexual."

"Ah."

"They've been together for a long time."

"Names."

Serenity rolled her eyes. She had always said Nicola could have been a drill sergeant.

"Adam and Mick."

"Hmm. Tell me."

"What?"

"There is something else you are holding back."

"How do you know that?"

Nicola sighed. "Because your voice changed when you said their names."

"What are you talking about?"

"It deepened."

Had it? "It did not."

She tsked. "You're just trying to stall."

She was. Serenity was sure at some point Jensen would call on Nicola for some reason or other. If she stretched the conversation out, she might be able to get out of an explanation.

"I have all the time in the world. Jensen's at a club, and you know what that means."

"Ah, and you didn't go?"

"Please. That man has no idea I live the lifestyle and I'm keeping it that way."

Both Nicola and her boss practiced bondage and submission, but he had no idea she did.

"Why?"

"It's my private life."

"And it gives you some kind of sick thrill that he doesn't know."

"And you're again trying to avoid the subject."

She sighed. "Okay, I'm sort of involved with them."

"Them? As in both of them?"

"Yes."

She whistled and Serenity had to hold the phone away from her ear. "Good lord, you know how to go all out. No dates for months, then you take on both men?"

She chuckled. "Believe me, I've had the same thought more than once, but...there is just something about them."

"What do you mean?"

"It's like, with them, I kind of feel complete."

"Wait. Are you playing with both of them at the same time? In bed together?"

"Yes."

"Look at you getting kinky."

"It's more than just being kinky. I know it sounds kind of corny, but together we seem to make sense."

Another beat of silence.

"Nicola?"

"Oh, sorry, I was just thinking."

"That's usually a bad sign."

"Shut up."

"Sorry."

"No, I was just thinking that I understand the situation."

"You understand the situation? You haven't even met them."

"Believe me, I *will* meet them in a few weeks. And I will get their last names from you so I can run a background check."

"You will not."

Another snort. "Try and stop me, little girl."

"Nicola."

"You know I am going to do it, but I will only look for criminal behavior."

Serenity rolled her eyes. "Okay."

"I was thinking about you though."

"Something about me screams ménage?"

"Don't be an idiot. Now, I don't want you to get irritated with me, but I always thought you were starving for love."

"Starving for love?"

"We talked about this before."

Nicola had been a sober companion and it spilled over into her personal life at times. "I had love from a lot of my fans."

"But not from the people who should have offered it up unconditionally."

Her parents. Her father had disappeared and her mother had used Serenity to make herself rich. In fact, she couldn't remember *ever* hearing her mother tell her she loved her.

"Serenity?"

She swallowed the lump in her throat. "Go on."

"You need a man who is going to love you to pieces, and getting involved with two men makes sense to me."

She rubbed her neck. "I don't know."

"What's wrong?"

"They overwhelm me at times. They've been together for over five years. Sometimes I feel like an interloper."

"Has either of them said anything to you about that?"

"No. It all happened so fast."

"Tell me about them."

"Mick is sweet. Well, as sweet as a former special forces guy who now works security can be."

"Jesus, you know how to pick them. And Adam?"

"Not as sweet, but there is this thick layer he uses to hide his vulnerability from the world."

She didn't say anything for a long time and that was a bad sign.

"Nicola?"

"Hmm, sorry. I was thinking."

"Thinking about what?"

"How long have you known these guys?"

"Over a month. Why?"

"You're in love with them."

Panic reached up and clawed at her throat. "I am not."
Was she?

"Yes, you are. You know them better than that one dude
you dated for six months."

"Huh. I hadn't even realized."

"That's because you're spending so much time falling in
love."

"I don't like that."

"What?"

"Falling in love."

"In general, or with these two men?"

"General, or both. Dammit, I don't know."

"Seri, don't panic." Her calm voice sent another wave of
anxiety rushing through her.

"I'm not." Not really. Her heart was just beating a
million beats per minute and she felt slightly ill.

"You're in love with two men who apparently like you."

"Yeah." She started to bite on her thumbnail as her mind
began contemplating all the problems with being in love with
two men.

"Serenity Jones," Nicola said in her drill sergeant voice.

"What?"

"Don't overthink this and don't freak out."

"I am not freaking out."

But she was. What if she was in love with them and they
weren't in love with her? What would happen then? She
would have her heart broken while they still had each other.

She sighed. "You are, but I know there is nothing I can
do about that. At least not all the way over here. Just don't

make any rash decisions. This isn't orthodox, but then, you never have been. As I said, these men might give you just what you need."

"I'll try." She sighed. "They like to play a bit too."

"Lord, two men, former special forces, and Doms? You definitely know how to take the leap, woman."

She chuckled. "True."

"Have you engaged?"

"No, not yet. They want to take me to some place called Rough 'n Ready."

"Yeah, good club. Micah Ross, the owner, is great. Jensen is a member too."

"Too? That means you're a member?"

"I was thinking about it. I mainly get a day pass most of the time. But, you're interested?"

"Yes. I've been reading a lot."

"Good. It's good for you to try new things, and it sounds like you trust these men."

Before she could work through the bombshell Nicola had just lobbed at her, Nicola said, "Okay, I have to go."

"I told you Jensen would come back."

"Ha, no. I have a *friend* who lives here. We're going to play a bit since I have the night off." Knowing Nicola, she had men all over the world just waiting for their favorite sub to return. "I'll call you with our itinerary when I get it. And Seri, call if you need to talk. Any time of the day or night. You know I'm here for you."

"I do. Thank you."

"Love you."

"Love you back."

They hung up and Serenity picked up her coffee again, only to find it cold. She went into the house to pour another cup, the conversation playing over in her mind. Nicola was right. She had always been starving for attention and love. It was what had led to her drinking and out of control behavior. More than one person had used her to get things they wanted, whether it was her connections in Hollywood, money, or just free crap. She had been so damned desperate to be accepted, she would have done anything at that point.

Since then, she'd been very careful not to let people know how much she needed that in her life. If she fell in with those people, she might lose control of her life again. This time she might not be able to come back from it whole.

Still, she didn't want to panic. They were having fun, and she was enjoying two interesting men who apparently found her interesting. She'd worry about the future later.

Nicola was right. She did trust them. From the very first, she had never felt threatened or used in any way. It's why she had been drawn to them to begin with. There was a solid core of good in them. She could depend on both men, no matter what.

And she wanted to find out what submission with these two men would be like.

With that thought, she sat down at her desk and started working on the pictures she had taken the week before. They wouldn't be back until tomorrow and she would tell them then.

twenty

T he day after they returned from Kauai, Mick was awake before the sun. He hadn't slept well, even with Adam beside him. He knew the reason.

As he poured his coffee, he glanced out the window toward Serenity's house. He had known she was special the first time they'd been together, but she was getting under his skin. After she had told them she wanted to sleep in her own bed, Mick and Adam had returned to their house. Neither of them had been happy about her decision.

She wasn't there and there was something missing.

It had never happened in their relationship. From the time they had moved into a sexual relationship, they enjoyed women, but they could also be together by themselves. Less than a month with Serenity, and they both felt the void.

"You're up early," Adam said.

He glanced at his lover. Sleepy eyes, bed head, and wearing nothing but a pair of board shorts. It was usually enough to get him going. But now, he wanted to share that with Serenity. She had become a part of their lives and now he was scared he'd made a mistake.

"Uh oh. That's a serious look."

"What's that mean?" Mick asked.

"It means that you're the pretty one. You don't worry."

He knew Adam was joking, but he couldn't help but feel irritated.

"And what are you?"

"The smart one."

When he didn't respond, Adam stopped. "What's up, babe?"

He shrugged and left the kitchen, walking out onto the back lanai. Adam soon followed, his coffee cup in hand.

He came up behind Mick, and rested his chin on his shoulder.

"Spit it out."

"What?"

"We have the day off together and I want to relax. I don't want this issue rearing its head. Whatever it is."

He sighed. Mick could fight him, then they would argue. In the end, he knew he would end up telling Adam.

"I think I'm getting too hung up."

"Understandable. I'm hot."

He rolled his eyes. "Now is not the time for you to get a sense of humor."

"See. I'm the smart one."

"Fuck," he said and sat down in one of the three chairs on the lanai.

Adam said nothing for a long moment, and it was the right thing.

"Sorry. Just...I didn't think she'd become so important so fast."

"Ah."

"Ah, what?"

"Listen, I'm worried about that too. But, with our relationship, it happened slowly. We knew each other years before we took that leap--thanks to a bottle of whiskey."

Adam smiled, thinking of their first night of R & R. They both had known each other were bisexual and after months of dancing around the idea, they had indulged. They had been together ever since.

"So?"

"While you like to pretend you are a free spirit, you're not. The idea of Serenity being a part of our lives scares you shitless."

"I am a free spirit."

Adam snorted. "Son, you are the farthest thing from it. You like to keep things light, but that doesn't make you a go with the flow type."

"And what type am I?"

"Home and hearth and happily ever after. With me, you knew you had it right off. Now, you aren't too sure. You love her, but there are no guarantees even after telling her. That makes you nervous."

Because he was a little too close to the truth, Mick rose out of the chair and walked to the railing. Yes, he was nervous but there was something under it that he wasn't comfortable with. Fear. His gut coiled. He was afraid that she would walk away. It would be easy for her. They had just been having fun, a little fling. But now, his heart was starting to engage.

Adam sighed behind him. "You've got to snap out of this funk, Mick."

He turned around to face Adam. From the moment they'd met, they had been fast friends. It had deepened into love. That part hadn't taken so long.

"I can see those wheels turning in your head."

"It doesn't bother you?"

"What?"

"Waiting around, knowing she could just walk away?"

"Yeah, it bothers me, but I think because of my childhood, I handle it better."

An abusive mother, absent dad, then a string of foster homes had been his entire childhood. No security and no long-lasting relationships.

"So, because I had a good childhood, I can't understand?"

He chuckled as he leaned forward, resting his forearms on his legs.

"In a way. I view life as temporary. This great life we built, it could all disappear."

"Damn. That's cynical."

He shrugged. "Maybe. But see, you had those parents of yours--"

"Ours."

He smiled and nodded. "Ours. They were there all the time."

"Dad was gone a lot."

His father had been a Green Beret, and he'd been deployed.

"Yeah, but they were there. And even if something happened to him, you knew your mother was going to be there for you. I never had that."

"And now you are a cynical bastard."

"Yeah, but there's something else. I've had to learn how to go with the flow more than you."

"You plan every damned minute of the day."

"No. I do not. I would not have ended up at Serenity's house last week. Completely unplanned. I plan, because it gives me comfort. Still, there is always a part of me that thinks it could all be blown to smithereens at any moment."

"You're all right with that?"

"No, but I know how to deal with it. Someone's been pulling the rug out from beneath my feet since birth. You, on the other hand, are a whiney ass titty baby, who had been treated like a prince for most of your life."

Laughter filled his voice, pulling a smile from Mick.

"Okay, yeah, I was a bit of a Mama's boy."

"I was thinking that maybe we should play tourist today."

"Sure, what do you have in mind?"

"Maybe some time at the beach. Get some shaved ice."

"We haven't been to Waikiki in a while."

"Oh, yeah. Lalani Coffee house for some pancakes, then beach time?"

Mick nodded. "Wanna ask Serenity?"

He nodded. "I think that's an excellent idea."

SERENITY DUG HER TOES INTO THE SAND AND sighed. It was just after eleven. Her belly was filled with pineapple pancakes and coconut syrup. There was a gentle trade wind keeping her cool, and the sun felt good on her flesh.

Oh, yeah, and she was with the two hottest guys on the beach.

"I can't remember the last time I came down here for a day of just sitting on the beach," she said.

"What are you usually doing?" Mick asked.

"Taking pics. I rarely miss an opportunity to work."

"That's a shame. You live in one of the most beautiful places on earth. You need to make sure to enjoy it," Adam said.

She knew he was right, and she did have some breathing room. With her online sales doing well, along with her possible book deal, she felt secure with her income. Granted, she still had money from her acting days, but she was careful with it.

"You're right. I tend to worry about missing something, but it is pretty near perfect almost three hundred and sixty-five days a year."

She picked up her sunscreen, but Mick took it out of her hands.

"Let me."

Oh, God, not good. He was going to drive her insane by touching her in public.

He settled in behind her and she listened as he squirted some of lotion on her back. He set the bottle down and started to rub it in. Just that simple touch had her nipples hardening. She was right. They had both turned her into some kind of a nympho.

"Adam told me he talked to you about Rough 'n Ready."

She nodded, unable to speak. His talented fingers slipped over her skin with all that lotion...well, there was only so much a girl could take. She drew her legs up and rested her head on her knees. She just thanked god she had her glasses on. Closing her eyes, she bit her lip to keep from moaning. Mick kept rattling on about the club and how they would get her a pass for the night, and she just wanted to turn around and jump his bones.

"Aren't you Kayleigh Rose?"

She straightened and looked at the young man. He was probably a decade younger than she was, skinny enough a strong wind would blow him away, and he had the tell-tale sign of a haole with a new tan.

She looked up at him trying to ignore the dangerous man behind her. Both men had straightened up and had their full attention on the newcomer.

"Kayleigh who?"

"You know, the *Daughter Knows Best* show. You *are* her."

"Nope. My name's Serenity Jones. But it happens a lot."

"Are you sure?"

She opened her mouth to respond, but, apparently, Adam had had enough.

"She said she isn't her."

The young man took a step back. Smart kid.

"No worries. I get people who think I am her all the time. Now if it came with perks, like free drinks, I might go with it, but I rarely get any offers."

"Oh, okay. Sorry."

"No problem," she said to his retreating back.

"You two should be ashamed of yourselves."

Adam barely glanced at her, then back to the young man, who was now halfway down the beach. "You need to be more careful. I didn't know you were *that* well known."

She shrugged, knowing she had left that part of her life out of most of their conversations on purpose. Apparently, the guys had decided not to snoop. "Not really. I haven't had an incident in years."

"An incident?" Mick asked as he started to rub lotion on her again.

"Yeah. When the show was doing really well, I would have to fight to keep my privacy. I had one person follow me into the bathroom and stick their camera under the stall door."

"Jesus."

"That really happened?" Adam asked.

She nodded. "It was not fun. It was one of the reasons I walked away from it all."

"But there were other reasons?"

She hated talking about it. Maybe that was why she rarely had close friends these days. Acquaintances didn't like to ask.

This was different. She was involved with them, and while she had a right to say no, she wanted them to know about that other life. She had kept it to herself for a long time, so it took her a moment or two to gather her courage to talk about it.

"Privacy was one big issue. I also saw the writing on the wall with my career."

"How so?" Mick asked, finishing off her back then taking his place beside her.

She thought back to the summer before she turned seventeen. She knew the show wasn't doing well, worse, she knew she was part of the reason.

"I was sixteen going on thirty." She glanced around and found that no one was paying attention so she continued. "I had to take uppers to just get out of bed. I was exhausted all the time. Partying all night and then working all day is never fun, even when you are teenaged."

"Easier than when you are thirty."

She chuckled. "True, but it was not a path to happiness. Uppers in the morning, coffee throughout the day, and alcohol at night."

"You were sixteen," Mick said.

"Yeah, well, I started drinking when I was thirteen or fourteen, so it was no big deal."

He made a sound of disgust and Adam laughed. "Forgive Mick. As wild as he can be, he grew up with a very strict father and a doting mother. He had nothing to escape."

"Don't get me wrong. I wasn't this poor abused child. Part of it was my fault. I knew just how to act out to get attention in the rags. So, there I was, acting on a show I hated, dealing with the life of a teenage actress who doesn't even want to get out of bed, and I snapped. I couldn't do it anymore. Worse, I knew I didn't want to act."

"So, you didn't want to act. What's wrong with that?"

"I had been brought up in front of the camera. I knew that I had nothing else to offer anyone, and worse, my mother had expectations. I'd been supporting my family since I was five years old."

"And I take it your mother wanted you to continue on?" Mick asked.

She nodded.

"She was working out deals for all these horrible movies. I started to see my future as a washed-up teen star, who was never that good at acting, being stuck working on movies that were embarrassing. Skin teen flicks. At one time, I had thought I wanted to be a serious actress. As I said, I hated acting by the time I left it."

"But you had liked it at one time?"

"Yeah. But, then, when you're five years old, and you have an entire crew to do your hair and dress you up, it's like play, you know. Especially if you were a girly girl."

"And I take it you were."

She smiled. "Yep. Even before my first commercial, I would happily sit for hours at a time to have my hair and nails done. As with everything else, though, it got to be a chore. It was no longer fun for me to go out. I couldn't just throw on anything and go to the store. There was always someone with a camera everywhere I went."

They were both looking at her as if she had grown another head. So, she decided to change the subject.

"So, Adam was telling me about this club you two go to."

Mick glanced between them, then settled his gaze on hers. "You want to go to Rough 'n Ready?"

She nodded. "I...well. I've read BDSM books, mainly romances. But, I'm a girl who has to see things and Adam offered a trip."

Mick looked between the two of them, then he smiled. "I've already talked to Ross and got a pass for you. How about tonight?"

"Sounds like a fantastic plan," she said.

twenty-one

They stepped through the door at Rough 'n Ready and Serenity blinked. It was such a contrast to Hawaii. A low thrum of music filled the room. In here, the lights were dim, but there was enough light to look around. There was a dance floor, which she hadn't expected to see, and seating. Booths lined the area by the bar. It was packed, even for a Sunday night.

She tapped Mick's arm and then motioned him to lean down. "Is it always this busy?"

"No. Sometimes it's even busier. They have the only BDSM club in the islands."

"Since we aren't playing, why don't we get a drink?" Adam said.

They led her to the bar with a petite brunet serving drinks. She glanced at their wrists.

"Not playing tonight, boys?"

"No," Mick said.

"Dee, this is our friend Serenity. Serenity, this is Dee."

The woman smiled. "Hey. Nice to meet you. So, you're the one who got the free pass."

"Uh, I guess so. Am I?"

Adam chuckled. "Don't worry. Micah owes us a few favors."

"Who is Micah?"

"My ears were hot and I was wondering why," a Southern accent came from behind her.

She turned and found a large Native American man wearing a pair of black jeans and a dress shirt. A long water-fall of black silky hair trailed down his back. And he was smiling at her. He had a pretty smile.

"Micah, this is Serenity," Mick said,

He took her hand and kissed the top of it.

"So, nice to meet you."

"Nice to meet you too. Thank you for the pass."

"As Adam said, I do owe them a few favors, and lord knows how many members they've helped add to my club."

He glanced over her shoulder toward the bar. "You look tired."

"I am not tired," Dee said.

"You should take a break."

"You should get bent."

He only smiled.

"My staff doesn't respect me. I thought maybe you would like the manager's table for tonight."

"Oh, I don't want to put you out."

"You're not putting me out." Then, he stepped toward

the bar and leaned over it. He pulled Dee forward and kissed her.

"Take a break."

She shook her head, but Serenity did not miss her smile. Micah held out his arm and waited until she took it.

"I think you should make sure to watch St. John tonight. He and his wife are over from Hawai'i doing a demonstration on spanking. Adam told me you are a novice?"

She nodded.

"If you decide to join as a member, we have a lot of classes. They take place in the club, but they aren't out in the open like this."

"Thank you."

They arrived at a u-shaped booth and he handed her up. "Enjoy yourself tonight, and like I said, make sure you watch Eli and his wife. They are very good at this."

The guys joined her.

"I take it he's involved with the bartender?" she asked.

Adam nodded. "Married. And from the way he's acting, they are going to have baby number three later this year."

"This St. John and his wife...when Micah says they are going to do a demonstration, he means naked?"

Mick chuckled. "Kind of hard to watch a spanking demonstration if she's wearing clothes."

She was both embarrassed and horribly intrigued by the notion.

"What?" he asked.

She shrugged. "I don't think I would ever do that. Not in public I mean."

"Not everyone has to, and not everyone wants to," Adam explained. "Some people it helps in their enjoyment of the scene they are performing. Others prefer to keep things private."

"And what would you two be?"

"Private," they both answered at the same time, which made her laugh. Just then a waitress stopped at the table and gave them their drinks.

As she sipped on her mai tai, she watched the crowd, she found herself intrigued. The crowd had lots of beautiful people, but also very ordinary folks.

"What are you thinking?" Mick said, his breath feathering over her ear.

"I'm thinking that these people are all normal."

"What did you expect?'

"I'm not sure. I partied a lot, but I was never adventurous in the bedroom."

"Ah. I will admit, there is always a strange one in every crowd, but you are right."

"Come here," Adam said as he urged her to set down her drink and slip closer to him.

And without any indication of what he had planned, he bent his head and kissed her. And not just a little peck on the cheek or brush of her lips. He slid his tongue over the seam of her lips. At the same moment, she felt Mick's mouth over her neck. She moaned and opened her mouth to Adam. And just like before, she was lost again. Every time they touched her, they were all that mattered. She could think of nothing else, not who might be watching, or that people might judge them for their relationship. She just wanted to feel.

Mick crowded in behind her as Adam cupped her face, deepening the kiss. She gasped in the next instant because she felt Mick's hands sliding over her hip, then to her breasts. Shifting in the seat, she aggravated her arousal even more. She'd almost gone without panties, but even so, she was damned sure her legs were probably dripping.

Apparently, Adam read her thoughts. He slipped his hand down her torso and eased her skirt up.

Oh, God.

He eased her legs apart with his hand and she was helpless to stop him. Why would any sane woman want to? Each time he brushed against her flesh, she had to fight back a moan. He wasn't aggressive. Every touch seemed to be measured. He eased her panties aside. The moment his finger slid against her slit, she almost came. She wanted to so badly, to just let loose and lose control. But Adam had other plans. He slipped his hand from between her legs and pulled away.

"What?"

"Not here. We said we don't like to play in public."

She frowned at him and looked over her shoulder at Mick. "So, this was just about teasing?"

"No," Adam said, drawing her attention to him again. He waited to continue until she looked at him. "This is about control. You want to play, you need to learn the rules."

She opened her mouth to complain, but he stopped her.

"No. Final word. Besides, the demonstration is about to start and it's something you should watch. If you decide to grant us this honor, then we need to know everything you desire, because it will be our job to give it to you."

She wanted to ask more, but she did as he asked. And maybe, she wouldn't go crazy waiting.

ADAM WAS TRYING TO CONTROL HIS NEEDS AS THEY found a place close to the viewing area. There were private rooms below, and then there were two or three that were used for demonstrations. They were situated on what was really the first level of the club. They were on the second level, which always felt like it was the first. Micah and his partner Ethan had designed it to give it that feel.

They had found a place close to the front of the crowd and like Micah had said, there were a lot of people interested. St. John was a big attraction, but now that he was married, Adam knew the two of them would whip the onlookers into a frenzy. The couple were so in tune with each other that it was mesmerizing.

It was going to be interesting to see Serenity's reaction to it. He had been happy when Mick said he could take the lead. They traded off, and sometimes, he was okay with Mick playing the Dom. Tonight though, he wanted to be the one. He knew they wouldn't go into a full-fledged submission.

None of them were ready for that.

He leaned forward so that his mouth was close to her ear. Drawing in a deep breath, he reminded himself to stay in control. It wasn't usually a problem for him. In fact, he was sometimes too controlled, or so Mick claimed. But with Serenity, it was different. As both he and Mick had acknowledged, this relationship wasn't the same as their previous threesomes.

He glanced over at his partner, who was watching the room below. As if sensing his study, Mick turned toward him. Each of them was wound tight. Adam leaned over and brushed his mouth over Mick's without either of them closing their eyes. They didn't know exactly what they had been looking for, but if this worked out with Serenity, they might have found a woman for the two of them.

There was a murmur that moved through the crowd, and he realized that the St. John's had entered the room. Eli was a big guy, no shirt, and damned leather pants that molded perfectly to his ass. But tonight, the woman drew his attention.

He'd met Crysta a time or two. She was tall, part African-American, part Hawaiian. She was already naked when they walked into the room. He turned back to Serenity and drew in another long breath. Sweet rose filled his senses. These days, that always aroused him. It was her, that flower scent mixed in with her own essence that could draw him in every time. He would immediately become aroused in the way he would when he detected sandalwood--Mick's favorite cologne.

Her gaze was fixed on the scene below, and while they didn't play in public, there was no reason that they couldn't start a little play in the club.

"Put your hands on the railing," he whispered in her ear.

She didn't even hesitate. She did as he ordered, her attention still on the couple below. St. John strapped his wife down then walked over to pick out his toy of choice.

"Hmm, which one do you like?"

"What?" Her voice shook when she asked the question.

"How would you like to be spanked? Just a bare hand? Or maybe a nice little flogger?"

"I haven't given it much thought."

"Liar. I know you have." That he didn't know, but he had an idea after the demonstration, she would be very interested in it.

"I think I would like the paddle."

"Hmm," was all he said as he lowered his head so he could taste her flesh. He pressed his mouth against the sensitive flesh just behind her ear, then he pulled her earlobe into his mouth. She shuddered and turned her head.

"Eyes forward, Serenity."

Again, like a good little sub, she did as he told her. How had this woman never taken the chance to learn about the lifestyle? She seemed perfectly suited for it.

He watched her watch the spanking. St. John had picked a paddle, Serenity's choice. The day before, another box of toys had arrived at the house, and he had cursed Mick for buying it. Now, though, the paddle, flogger, and crop seemed like perfect timing.

The first hit of the paddle against Crysta's ass sounded through the club. For the demonstration, the St. John's had requested no music. Serenity's breath caught. If he hadn't been paying so much attention to her, he would have missed it. Each whack of the paddle heightened her arousal. It was easy to see. Her breathing increased and he watched her pulse beat harder in her neck. She licked her lips and transferred her weight back and forth between her feet.

"Stop moving."

She made an irritated sound, but she did as he asked.

Now it was time to turn up the heat. She needed to understand just what she would gain from submitting to them.

"No moving, unless I tell you. Nod if you understand?"

She nodded.

"Keep your eyes on them. You like that. I can tell. I want to paint a picture of what we can offer. What I think you need."

She drew in a deep breath.

"We both like to spank. A woman who likes to be spanked gets so fucking wet. Just watching it has you dripping, doesn't it?"

She nodded.

"Your nipples get tight, your pussy drips and you are going to want to come, but see, we control that too. We give you permission, and we don't like to do anything quickly, but you already know that, don't you?"

He slipped his hand over her hip, allowing his fingers to linger over her. He knew talking to her like this was turning her on, but he had trapped himself. With each sentence, he saw her reaction, felt it in his core. That only spurred his own arousal. Mick was going to have to drive home.

"Would you like to try that, Serenity? Would you like us to spank you?"

She nodded.

"Would you like to go now?"

She nodded again.

"Well, not just yet. Look, St. John is getting the flogger."

St. John started using it. With each smack against her ass, Crysta moaned.

"Oh, yeah, she likes that. Just like you will."

She said nothing, but she shuddered again. The motion had her ass pressing against his cock.

Fuck.

Adam looked over at Mick and found him watching them. He saw the intensity in Mick's eyes and decided it had been long enough.

"Want to go, pet?"

She nodded.

"What will you give me?"

"What?"

"You want to leave, you need to offer me something. How about you suck my cock with that perfect little mouth of yours?"

"Now? Here?"

Damn, she sounded like she wanted to do that, but he had been honest before. They liked their privacy.

"No, but I think we need to go."

It wasn't too hard to get out of the club. Everyone's attention was on the demonstration. They worked their way through the crowd, then out into the sultry night air.

After crossing the street, they found the SUV. Mick climbed into the driver's seat and Serenity moved to step in. Adam stopped her. He slipped his finger beneath her chin and urged her to look at him. Her eyes were hazy with arousal.

"Are you sure you want to do this? You can say no right now, and there will be no hard feelings."

"Yes."

"I need a safe word. We aren't going to do anything radical tonight, but just in case you are overwhelmed, I want you to have a way out."

"Blue."

He nodded. "Take off your panties."

Her eyes widened.

"Take them off," he said, this time a little more forcefully.

She looked around, but then complied with his orders.

"Put them in the front seat. That way Mick can see them."

She placed them on the front seat, then closed the door.

"Now, in you go, all the way to the back."

He followed her into the vehicle and they were soon on their way.

"Push your skirt up to your hips and spread your legs."

After she did, he reached over and pressed his hand against her pussy and groaned.

"Wet?" Mick asked from up front.

"Fucking dripping."

He caressed her, teasing her clit and dragging his index finger against her slit. Her breathing increased, and he could

197

tell she was already close to losing her control. He stopped moving.

"Rules for right now. You may not come." Her gaze locked on his. "I mean it, Serenity, no coming."

She nodded.

Once he had her agreement, he started to move his hand again. Over and over, he pushed her to the edge, only to pull away when she almost came.

She bit her lip.

"No. Let me see your pleasure. Let me hear it. I need to know what you want."

"I want to come."

He slapped her pussy. "No. And for asking, I think I deserve a little of that payment."

He pulled his hand away and unzipped his pants. Her gaze focused on his cock and she licked her lips. The woman was going to kill him.

Once he had her situated where he wanted her, he said, "Suck."

She reached for him.

"No hands. Just all mouth. Put your hands behind you back. And, Serenity, if you make me come, you swallow it all, understand?"

She nodded. He held his cock up.

"Lick my balls first."

She did, sliding the tip of her tongue over his flesh, then he held his cock by the base to make it easier for her. She took him in, swirling her tongue over his cock, grazing the tip of it with her teeth.

"Fuck. That mouth of yours is fucking lethal."

She gagged a couple of times, but she ignored it. He watched, mesmerized by her bobbing head.

"Oh, yeah, that's good, just like that, Serenity."

He started to thrust up into her warm, wet mouth. Each time pushed him closer to his orgasm. Once...twice...

He closed his eyes as the rush of his orgasm took control of his every thought. He thrust hard up into her mouth, shuddering as pleasure rushed through him. She drank him in, swallowing and then pulling back to lick over the head of his penis.

"God, that was good."

He leaned forward and kissed her just as Mick pulled onto the little road that lead to their houses.

He helped her out of the car and then carried her into the house. Mick led the way to their bedroom, stopping off in the kitchen to grab a couple of waters. Once they were in the bedroom, he set her on her feet.

"Before we go on, there are rules. We control your pleasure. Tonight, I am mainly in charge, but you must listen to Mick also, do you understand?"

She nodded.

"Good. You do not have to do anything you don't want to. This is a safe place, as always. We want to give you pleasure, but you can't have pleasure if you are scared. You use your safe word or just say no. Tonight, we are planning on just a little spanking and no more submission than I asked for in the SUV." He drew in a deep breath, and tried to read her expression. "You can say no now and we walk away. No hard feelings and Mick and I will understand. At any time it is too much, you can call a stop to it."

"I understand."

"We just want to be sure since you are a novice. Some new subs feel that if they say no, then their Dom will lose interest and that is not true. This is just another level of our relationship. Still willing?"

She nodded.

He stepped back and took one of the two chairs they had in their bedroom. Mick sat down in the other. Serenity stood in front of the bed, looking aroused and worried.

"First things first, we need to get you naked."

twenty-two

Serenity stood before them and fought off the shiver. She wasn't cold or even scared. White hot need poured through every vein in her body. She wanted this so badly and from her play in the car with Adam, she was beyond ready for sex.

She clenched her thighs together.

"Stop that," Adam said.

"What?"

"Pressing your legs together. It gives you a little relief. In fact," he said as he walked toward her, "take one step out with each foot."

She hesitated.

"Do it now, Serenity."

She did as he ordered.

"Good, pet."

He'd never used that name before, and she had a feeling it had to do with the situation. Normally, she hated it. It was one of those names that made her cringe. Something was different right now. It made her hotter.

He stepped up beside her and eased her skirt up. "Do you think you deserve a pet, pet?"

She swallowed and nodded.

"Mick?"

"A little one," he said as he started to undress.

"Hmm, I guess so," Adam said, reaching between her legs and sliding a finger along her dripping slit. "So wet. It must be killing you right now." He gave her pussy a pat, then moved away. It was barely enough to give her any kind of relief. If anything, it ratcheted up her arousal. He walked over to Mick and held his finger up to Mick's mouth. Mick opened his mouth and let Adam slip his finger into his mouth.

Oh, damn.

"So fucking tasty," Mick said, arousal humming in his voice. "But, then, you always are."

He sat down in one of the easy chairs they had against the wall opposite the bed.

"So, pet," Adam said. "I would like to see you naked."

Hot damn, she was ready for that. Her hands went to the bottom of her shirt, but he smacked them away.

She frowned at him.

"First me. I want you to take my clothes off. And it isn't going to be that hard. I'm already unzipped."

He stood in front of her.

"Take my shirt off first. Wait." He moved them so that they were standing in profile for Mick to see. "Better, Mick?"

"Oh, yeah," he said, as he wrapped his hand around his cock and gave it a long tug. Then he settled back to watch.

"Now, my shirt."

She was standing there, her body so damned hot she was amazed she hadn't passed out, her ass hanging out because her skirt was around her waist, and her hands were shaking. Somehow, she was supposed to figure out how to unbutton his shirt.

She reached up and started on her task. It took her a couple of tries, but she finally got the first one undone. She made quick work of the others.

"Someone tells me that she's ready for some down and dirty sex," Mick said with a laugh as Adam's shirt fell to the floor.

He tsked. "Pick it up, pet. Fold it, and place it on the empty chair."

She stepped around him and did as he asked. She felt the rough palm of his hand against her ass and she shivered. Still, she completed the task and returned to him.

"Good. Now, the pants. "

She did that, helping him step out of them, then folding them and placing them on top of his shirt.

"Oh, what a good little sub," Mick said, admiration threading his voice. She didn't know why, but she had to fight the smile that threatened to curve her lips.

"Now, you're still clothed and I want to see that pretty body of ours."

She turned to face them. They were both fully aroused, ready to go. Good, because she needed them right now. Her body was vibrating with need for them both. She wanted to offer herself up to them to do whatever they wanted. She didn't care what happened at this point.

"Slip off that skirt and your shirt. I want you completely naked, so take off your bra too," he said as Mick stood up. He went to their walk-in closet and retrieved a wooden box. Her gaze followed him as he came back out and she got a smack on her ass.

She frowned at Adam.

"Eyes on me."

She thought she heard Mick chuckle but she wasn't sure. Her ass was still stinging from the smack, plus it had heightened her arousal.

"Tonight, we just want to do a little playing. Nothing too much. You have an interest in spankings, and we like to do that. A lot. So, we will do that. Turn and face the bed, pet. Place your hands on the mattress and stick that beautiful ass out for us to see."

She didn't hesitate. Once she was in position, Adam rubbed his hand over her ass.

"Beautiful."

"Yes," Mick said. "I can't wait to sink into her."

The stark need in his voice heightened her senses.

"Oh, pet likes that kind of talk, doncha?" Adam asked as his finger tailed down her crease to her sexy pussy. "Damn, you're even wetter."

She should be embarrassed, but right now, she didn't care. He was teasing her with his fingers, and she was so damned close. She made the mistake of swiveling her hips.

"Bad, Serenity," Adam said, as he pulled his hand from between her legs. "I think she needs to remember what the rules are, Mick."

"Oh, yeah," he said and she heard some movement. She didn't dare turn around. Mick stepped up beside her and leaned down to kiss her. "Remember your safe word."

She nodded. Then, he straightened and without warning, he smacked her with a paddle. She drew in a swift, deep breath.

When she said nothing else, Mick continued, over and over, smacking her ass. The pain of it dissolved into pleasure as the heat of the paddling filtered out over her flesh. She didn't come, just as Adam had ordered her, but she knew her thighs were wet with her desire.

"Shit, Adam."

"I know," Adam said. She felt his fingers dancing over her sensitive skin. "So pretty." Then he slid his fingers down her ass. He played with her puckered hole before he slipped inside. Instantly, she clamped down on his digit. Delightful shivers rolled through her as she felt herself moving closer to the edge.

"Oh, fuck, she's so close," Adam ground out. He leaned down closer. "Not yet, Serenity. We aren't done with you."

She almost lost it then. Her whole body seemed to be overly sensitive to every element in the room. She was hot and perspiring, but the cool AC air danced over her skin. Even that made her think about coming. Hell, a bird could chirp and she would feel like coming.

Mick picked her up and set her on the bed.

"Up on all fours," he said.

Once she was in position, he moved her forward so that she was on the edge of the mattress. Then he took his cock in one hand and held it close to her mouth. Precum wet the head, and she could almost taste the salty, sweet essence.

"Open up," he said.

She already had her mouth open before he finished the sentence. He chuckled as he slid his cock between her lips and started to fuck her mouth. He molded his hand to the back of her head as he thrust deeper and deeper into her mouth. As he did, she felt the bed dip behind her, but she paid no attention. She continued to suck Mick. Each time he bumped against the back of her throat, she enjoyed it even more.

Adam spread her legs out a little, and set the vibrator against her pussy. She shuddered, trying her best to continue to deep throat Mick. She wanted to taste his cum, have it slide down her throat. But, he had other ideas. Adam increased the speed of the vibrator, Mick pulled out of her mouth. He slid his hand around to cup her face and kiss her.

"Not yet. I want to be deep in your ass when I come, Serenity. I want to feel all those muscles around my cock telling me we are together in our pleasure."

It pulled another shudder from her, and she felt her breast sway with the movement. Adam cupped them, then pinched both of her nipples.

Adam continued teasing her with the vibrator, changing the speeds over and over to push her even closer, but did not allow her to come.

The last time he turned down the speed, she moaned in pain. She physically hurt from not being able to come.

"I think it's time," Mick said.

Adam held the vibrator in place but he leaned closer to her. She felt the heat of him against her back. His breath whispered against her ear.

"Do you want to come, Serenity?"

She nodded.

"Say please, pet."

It took all her control not to scream at him. "Please."

"Good."

Serenity thought he would make her come by pushing the vibrator to a higher speed, but he removed the vibrator from between her legs. She heard foil wrappers and then Adam moved away, then returned. Mick picked her up as Adam slipped beneath her body.

"Do you need to come, pet?" he repeated.

She nodded.

"Not yet, but we'll get you there."

He lifted her up and thrust inside of her with one swift movement. The intrusion sent her closer to the edge, but she didn't go over. Mick climbed on the bed behind her and spread her ass cheeks. He eased into her passage as Adam waited.

Just like the times before, she felt so full with both men inside of her, delightfully so. But there was another layer of sensitivity this time around. They had always known how to push her buttons, and push her to the edge. This time, though, it was different. It was so much more. More sensitive, more need, more everything. Their denying her orgasm for so long heightened all her senses and had her ready to do anything for them.

They started to move within her. Damn, every cell of her body seemed to come alive in anticipation. Their movements started out measured and she found herself frustrated. Then, though, they seemed to move past some barrier where both men increased their speed. This was different than before. She felt different. Everything seemed to shift. It was more intense. Every shift of their bodies against hers and the way they felt as they thrust inside of her made her feel even more connected to them.

Adam nipped at her throat, his teeth grazing over her flesh. He had done things like that before, but again, it affected her more this time. As their thrusts grew more powerful, Mick smacked her ass. Her skin was still sensitive from their paddling, but the feel of Mick's bare hand against her ass was even better now. She felt her pussy and ass clamp down tight on both men.

"Oh, fuck," Adam muttered. "Keep doing that, Mick. She likes it."

Mick did as Adam had ordered. Each time his hand connected with her skin, she felt her inner muscles tighten, her arousal soar. Their bodies were slick with their effort, and she didn't know how much longer she could hold on.

Adam cupped her face.

"Look at me, Serenity."

It took some effort but she opened her eyes.

"You need to come?"

She nodded, biting her lip.

"Come for us, baby. Do it."

Before he finished the order, she was coming. Her body shook as pleasure consumed her. She was so lost in her own orgasm, she barely noticed when both men shouted. She was still coming as they both thrust into her one last time. First Mick, then Adam stilled. She did not. She continued to convulse as the power of her release consumed her.

Long moments later, she collapsed. Mick moved away from her, and Adam wrapped his arms around her. She felt herself drifting off as the bed dipped beside them. Mick helped her off Adam and pulled her in for a cuddle. Adam left the bed for a moment, but returned. He snuggled up behind her.

"I love you guys," she said.

Mick kissed her forehead. Adam kissed her shoulder.

"We love you too, Serenity," Adam said.

It was the last thing she remembered before falling asleep.

twenty-three

I t had been a few weeks since she'd made it to the Kailua Farmer's Market, so Serenity bullied both Mick and Adam into going the next morning. Mick had been happy to go, but Adam had made excuses. His main one was for them to spend the day in bed. She knew he wanted to explore more of her submissive needs. Hell, she did too. They had already had another session in the early morning hours, but she also wanted to be normal. She wanted a relationship that was outside of the bedroom. When she explained it to Adam, he had no issues at all after that.

"Have y'all ever been here before?" she asked as she handed Adam a bag of goodies from one of the stalls.

"No. We had quite a few of our own trees at the last place. Some mango and papaya," Mick said.

She nodded. "I've thought about planting my own garden. But then, if you plant one, I can just poach."

Adam and Mick both laughed, but as their laughter

faded, she felt an itch between her shoulder blades. She rolled her shoulders trying to get rid of it.

"Something wrong?" Mick asked.

"No. Just...it's nothing."

In the old days, she would have been ducking and hiding. It was the tell-tale intuition that told her someone was watching her, usually paparazzi. This was Hawaii. No one knew who she was, or who she had been. Still, something crawled over her neck, warning her that someone was watching her.

She pushed the idea away. Again, it was Hawaii and that was a lifetime ago. Maybe, it was because she wondered how many people knew she was in a ménage relationship.

"So, I was thinking we could grab some shrimp on the way home and you could make us some shrimp truck shrimp."

She batted her eyes at Mick, who laughed.

"Sure. It would be nice to have dinner on the lanai."

She nodded, but the itch was back. Not wanting to alarm the guys over something that was her imagination, she pushed her worries aside.

"Hey, what about getting some malasadas too?" Adam asked.

"You are not good for my waistline," she said.

He slipped his arm around her waist and pulled her closer. The move surprised her because Adam wasn't the most openly affectionate in public. But, today, he didn't seem to have a problem.

He leaned down to whisper in her ear. "But I am so good at so many other things I do to you."

His breath was hot against her ear. She shivered. Right there in the middle of the market, she felt her hormones come to life, her nipples harden, and when she took a step, she realized her panties were slightly damp.

Adam apparently picked up on her reaction.

"You like dirty talk in public. I kind of like that. Maybe a public submission is in your future," he said as he tugged on her earlobe.

Mick smacked him up against his head. "Cool it."

The reverse roles the two men took right now almost made her laugh. Adam was usually the more sedate one, making sure to behave a certain way in public. Mick usually liked to push the limits.

She did chuckle then.

"First, I do as many good things to both of you. And secondly, I have no problem with affection in public as long as it doesn't go into a sex education demonstration. There *are* limits."

Adam smiled and Mick shook his head.

"Why don't you two grab the malasadas, but don't get any with the filling. Or, not all of them with the filling. I like the plain sugar ones. I'm going to take some pics around here."

Mick looked at Adam, who nodded and went off in search of the malasadas.

"I can't be on my own?"

"It's not that," Mick said. "Just that the two of us don't

need to be there to shop. Also, watching you work is kind of a turn on for me."

She glanced at him, then pulled out her camera. "That's a new one."

"Guys don't like your job?" he asked, his voice filled with surprise.

She shook her head. "Most of them were completely ambivalent to it, but many of them really didn't like me pulling out the camera. One of them said that I wasn't paying any attention to him."

"That's what is so sexy. You concentrate on something completely." He hummed. "It's so damned hot."

She stopped what she was doing and looked at him. "Really?"

He nodded. He had his aviator type sunglasses on and she couldn't see his eyes, but she was sure his gaze was boring into her. Heat flared in her belly. The tag team these two men did to her was so damned overwhelming at times. But even when they did—like at that very moment—she didn't think she would ever get enough.

"Let's just get these pictures done and then we can talk all about that."

"Yes ma'am."

SERENITY HUMMED AS SHE LOOKED OVER THE pictures she had taken the day before. It had been a week since the guys had told her they loved her. They hadn't pressured her to define what she felt for them past what she had already said. In other relationships, she would have worried about it. With Mick and Adam, she found a new sense of easiness.

She pulled up a pic she had taken of the two of them, on their lanai, sitting side by side, two beers on the table, their feet up on the table.

She moved onto the second pic, which showed them leaning over the table and kissing. It was almost innocent looking, but just seeing them together made her hot. How had she not known two men together was such a turn on for her? It might not just be men, but these men in particular.

Before she could follow that thread of thought, her phone rang. It was a California number so she clicked ignore. She knew it wasn't the guys or Nicola, so there was no reason to answer.

"Hey," Adam shouted from outside. She glanced toward the window and saw him standing on the path that led to the beach.

"Were you raised in a barn? You just yell at me from outside?"

He laughed. "Come on. Let's go watch the waves."

She glanced at her computer, then back to the man who was smiling at her. The man absolutely won out.

She shut down her computer, then joined him. He had snacks, which was always a plus.

"What do you have?"

"I got some malasadas and coco puffs."

She forgot about work, and everything else. "You win the day."

IT WASN'T UNTIL SHE RETURNED FROM THE BEACH that she remembered the phone call and message that had been left for her. She hit speaker.

"Hello, Ms. Jones. My name is Franklin Reynolds, an editor with the National Tattler." Her heart almost stopped beating. It had been one of the rags that had made her life a living hell. "I was wondering if I could get a quote about a story we are running this week that you are actually Kayleigh Rose. Also, it seems you have a unique relationship with two men. Please give me a call."

He rattled off the phone number, but Serenity barely noticed. Her entire world had just exploded. She had spent so many years in hiding that the idea of someone finding out who she was had been ludicrous. During the dark times after she ran from Hollywood, she had thought for sure she would be found out. Now that she was happy, finally on the right track with her life, and this crap had to happen.

Numb. It was the only feeling she had, as if she was in some form of shock. Of course, she was in shock. She had remained anonymous for over a decade.

Her phone rang in the silence, shocking her. It was Nicola.

"Hey," she said. "What the hell is going on?"

"What do you mean?"

"I just got a call from your mother trying to confirm your new name and that you are living in Hawaii."

She closed her eyes and panic started to set in. Her mother. *Dammit.*

"I...I have no idea. I just got a message from the National Tattler asking about this."

"Okay, let me make a few calls and maybe I can get the story suppressed."

"They don't just know my name. They know about Mick and Adam."

Oh, God, she sounded like she was losing it. What was she thinking? She *was* losing it. No one would blame her. The life she'd perfectly crafted. Now, it was going to be blown to smithereens.

"They know who you are?"

"Yes, they know. You know I really don't hide it from people. Just, I like the anonymity and keeping away from my mother. But this will be different. It's something to know the woman you were involved with had another career at one time. It is going to be something else when our lives are splashed all over the tabloids. The guys are going to hate me."

Serenity's voice had risen with each word, Nicola sighed. "Still, I'll bring the full force of Wulf Industries down on them. But you need to prepare your men."

"I don't think the rag has their names."

"But they will soon if we don't stop this. Let me make those calls."

"No. Please, I don't want you getting into trouble with Jensen."

"There is no problem with Jensen. Right, Jensen?"

"Off with their heads," he yelled out.

She smiled. "Thank you. I will owe you...again."

"Friends don't owe. They just love."

And that summed up their relationship. Nicola had been an Olympic hopeful with little interaction with people. They were alike in that regard. Granted, Nicola had had a loving family, but both women had spent their childhoods in isolation from their peers. "You sure they don't have Mick and Adam's names?"

"Not sure. They just said they knew I was in a relationship with two men."

"Hmm, well, don't call them. I will. No one messes with my Seri."

She smiled. "Thanks. I guess I have to talk to the guys."

"Yes, prepare them."

Dread filled her. This wasn't something she wanted to do. *Ever.* "Yeah, you're right."

"I'll call you back after I get through fucking up this rag."

Then she hung up. Even with the horrible news, Serenity found herself smiling. Nicola was tall, graceful, and the quintessential idea of a skater. She looked like a princess from another time. When she cussed, she was really pissed, and usually it made Serenity giggle. Today, it barely brought out a smile. The idea of what she had to do weighed heavily on her. With a sigh, she headed over to the guy's house.

There was music playing. She could hear it before she reached the lanai. When she reached the front door, she slipped off her slippahs, then knocked. Mick turned and smiled at her.

"You know you don't have to knock."

"Yeah," she said, knowing that more than likely, she would have to after today.

"Hey, what's wrong?" he said. Adam came out from the bedroom.

"What's up?"

She said the words she never wanted to say to either one of them.

"I have something to tell you."

twenty-four

Adam watched as Serenity sat down at the breakfast bar. The serious expression on her face was one he didn't think he had ever seen before. She looked as if her entire world had just fallen apart. His stomach muscles tightened. This was not going to be good news.

"I got a call today."

"The one when we were on the way to the beach?" Mick asked.

She nodded. "I let it go to voicemail. I just listened to it."

He shared a look with Mick, then they both looked at her again.

"What happened? Did someone die?"

She shook her head as her eyes filled.

"It was from the National Tattler. They know about us."

"What?" Adam said, trying to come up with a reasonable explanation in his own head. "They know about us? Us three?"

"Yeah, why do they care about that?" Mick asked.

She swallowed and looked away as if trying to gather the courage. He wanted to rush to her side and comfort her. Adam had the idea that she was too fragile—as if she would shatter if he touched her. When she looked back at them, her expression made his heart drop. She looked so sad and alone.

"I told you I changed my name when I was sixteen. That I was in the entertainment industry, remember?"

They both nodded.

"My real name was Kayleigh Rose Michaels. I went by Kayleigh Rose."

He had heard the name. Knew there were bad things associated with it, but he couldn't put his finger on the story.

"Kayleigh Rose? As in the teenage star of *My Sister Sam* and *Daughter Knows Best*?" Mick asked.

"Yes. You heard the guy at the beach. You knew I was on shows."

"Yeah, but it just didn't click." He knew that wasn't true. "You...you got in a lot of trouble."

She nodded. "I was headed to a short slide into drugs if I didn't walk away. I told you, I emancipated myself."

"You were the tabloid queen at the time."

She closed her eyes and nodded. When she opened them again, tears spilled down her cheeks. "Yes. I hate that term, but I was. I wanted to do everything bad. I was hell bent on ruining my life."

"And so, they found you?" Adam asked.

"Of course, they did," Mick said, irritation dripping from every word.

"What does that mean?" she asked.

"Maybe you wanted a little publicity so that you could get an extra big advance for that book you're planning. A story like this would definitely garner attention."

He looked at Mick. "Come on. You know she didn't do it."

"I don't know anything. You hid all this shit from us for a few months. But that was your plan all along."

"I didn't try to start up with you. You pursued me, if you recall."

Mick jerked a shoulder.

"I knew this would happen. You are no different than all the others."

"Hey, babe," Adam said and approached her, but she held up her hand.

"No. Just no." She drew in a deep breath. "My friend Nicola has already been called and, more than likely, my mother will find out about where I am. But Nicola is going to take care of things, or try."

"And how can she do that? Call a press conference for you?"

The sad look on her face dissolved into anger. "No. She works for Wulf Industries and is bringing down hell and damnation on those involved in this. Hopefully, she can keep them from running the story."

"She can do that?" Adam asked.

"She's Jensen Wulf's assistant, so yeah, there's a very good chance she can do exactly that."

He opened his mouth to tell her it would all work out, but true to form, Mick was losing his shit.

"Fat lot of good that's going to do. The story's out there."

"Jesus," she said, her voice rising. "It isn't out there yet."

"What do you care? You'll win out in the end."

"Oh, is that a fact?"

"Yeah."

Adam opened his mouth again to try and calm the argument, but Mick had hit a sore spot for Serenity and she went after him.

"Yeah, that's exactly what I want. I have spent the last decade under another name just so I could come out once I started a relationship with two men. Actually, that was my plan from the beginning."

"Babe," Adam said, but she shot him a dangerous look. He had to fight the need to step back from her. "Don't. You don't have the right anymore."

He wanted to protest, but he had a feeling that if he did, he would end up breaking her. She had a coat of armor on, but he had a feeling she was very close to losing it.

He nodded and she turned on Mick.

"Do you want to know why I left? Why I changed my name?"

"I don't really give a f--"

She held up her hand. "No. I got to hear all about your precious feelings, now you are going to know what my life was like. I had my first job when I was five. I remember thinking it was just for play. Then it became a job. When my father walked out, my mother had been desperate. She real-ized I could make money and she didn't have to do a damned thing, so she started pushing me. When I understood that if I didn't get a job, we would lose our apartment or maybe we just would go without eating for a day or two, I started having panic attacks. My mother got me a prescription for valium. I was eight."

Jesus.

"It got worse, you know. I was never a daughter, but a commodity. I worked, she lived the good life. I know now, looking back at it, if I hadn't made it in the legitimate indus-try, I would have probably ended up in porn when I turned eighteen. Well, I hope she would have waited until I turned eighteen. Either way, she wanted a certain lifestyle and she wanted me to provide it."

"Serenity," Adam breathed her name out.

"Don't you pity me."

"I don't pity you."

He glanced at Mick, who said nothing. His face was expressionless.

"Either way, the end of the whole entire deal came the morning I woke up in the hospital. See, at sixteen, I felt washed up. My show was being canceled. They hadn't told my mother, and I didn't want to tell her. I didn't want it to be another disappointment that she could hold over my head. So, after work, I went home and swallowed half a bottle of that valium she had supplied."

"You..."

"They said I was dead for a few seconds. Truth is, if

Nicola hadn't shown up to check on me, I would have died. And I wanted to be dead. See, I didn't want to think about what I would have to do next. What horrible thing I would be forced to do and live with later. I wanted it to go away. I was sixteen years old and I felt as if I had failed at life.

So, that morning, my mother showed up in the hospital."

"Wait, didn't you live with your mother?"

"We had an apartment she never slept at, so basically, I lived by myself."

His life had sucked. His mother had been a crack whore who had liked to beat on him, but she had never turned him out to make money. And that is what Serenity's mother did to her. She hadn't turned her into a whore, but she had used her own daughter to provide her a living, which was just as bad in his opinion.

"She wasn't happy with me. She said that if the tabloids found out about my *mistake*--that's what she called it--that I would be ruined. She berated me, called me a failure. That was before Nicola walked into the room. She read my mother the riot act and kicked her out."

"Nice story," Mick said, in his asshole voice. Adam hated the voice and knew what it meant. Mick was in a dark place.

"Not particularly, but it tells you something. I do not *ever* want that bitch to find me. I don't want to be a household name. I want to be who I am right now. And the woman I am right now has one message for you."

"What?"

"If you loved me like you said, you would have *never*

thought I would have done this to someone *I* loved. To two someone's I loved. So, please, by all means, go fuck yourself."

With that, she turned on her heel and headed out the door. He wanted to go after her, but Adam knew there was one person who needed him more right now, and that was Mick.

"What the hell was that about, Mick?"

"What?"

"What? Jesus, you really are an idiot. And this is so typical of you. You get all excited about something, and when everything doesn't go particularly perfect, you decide to blow it the fuck up."

"I'm not the one with the secret past."

"Secret past? What the hell? We're a freaking soap opera now."

He opened his mouth, but Adam had heard enough. "You do realize that you could have checked her out at any time before and during the relationship? With our connections, you could have easily found out everything about her. Hell, we probably could have googled her name and found her. After that guy said *Daughter Knows Best* on the beach, did either of us investigate? No. We didn't."

"I didn't want to."

"Nope, you sure didn't. You wanted her to be perfect, and in your eyes, for a while, she was. Now though, you think she did something, that she somehow brought this on herself."

"You make it sound like she's a victim."

"No, she's a survivor. She accomplished it the only way a sixteen-year-old could. And she has thrived."

"You sound like you admire her."

"Yes, I do, but this is more about identifying with her. You have no idea what a shitty childhood is like. I do. I know what it's like to have a parent who doesn't give a shit about you. I know the feeling of worthlessness that wells up inside of you. I'm thirty-three years old and I still have to deal with it. Not every day, but more often than I would like to admit."

"Adam," he said, his eyes widening. "I had no idea."

"How could you? You grew up in the safe shelter of Estelle McGrath. She made sure you had food. I bet you never worried about eviction notices either. Think about things from Serenity's perspective."

He crossed his arms over his chest. "I can't. She lied."

"Oh, Jesus."

He needed to step away because there was a chance he would punch Mick if he stayed. Neither of them needed that. But someone did need him.

Turning, he strode to the door.

"Where are you going?"

"I'm going to check on Serenity and leave you some time to deal with being a complete and utter asshole."

He left without waiting for Mick's answer.

As he hurried over to Serenity's house, he texted Estelle. They both needed a heads up just in case the scandal did hit the tabloids. He knew that her sweet baby boy wouldn't think to let her know. He would think about it later, but Adam knew Mick wasn't prepared to just now.

He sent the text just as he stepped up on Serenity's lanai. That's when he heard her. Quiet sobs filled the air. The soft sound broke his heart even more. This pain came out of her childhood. He understood. Show any kind of weakness and your enemy could use it against you. Only, for a neglected and abused child, their enemy was the person who should have been their protector. He kicked off his shoes, and without knocking, he stepped inside of her house. She wasn't in her front room, so he had a feeling she was in the bedroom. He followed the sounds of her weeping and found her curled up on her bed. She was facing away from him.

If Adam had any doubts whatsoever of his feelings for her, they would have ended right then and there. His chest fucking hurt.

"Serenity."

"Please, just go away."

Instead of arguing with her, he walked around so he could see her face. It was red and her eyes were puffy and still filled with tears.

"I can't go."

"Yes, you can. Just turn around and go back to that idiot."

He chuckled. "He is an idiot. If I go back right now, I'll punch him."

He wanted her to laugh, but instead, a fresh wave of tears filled her eyes. "I'm sorry. You should go back to him. I couldn't bear it if I broke you apart."

He couldn't wait any longer. He pulled her forward,

picked her up, then he sat down on the bed with her on his lap. He was happy when she didn't try to get away from him.

"You could never break us up. If we did break up, it would be on us, not you. Secondly, when Mick gets like this, you just need to leave him be. I've discovered that if you push, he pushes back."

She sniffed. "It isn't like him at all."

"Yes, it is. You've only seen happy Mick. He has some dark moments, and it often happens when he realizes that life isn't perfect."

She opened her mouth, but his phone rang.

"That's Mom."

"Your mother?"

"Our mother, but Mick's by blood."

"Why did you call her?"

"Because no one can kick her baby boy's ass like a military mom. And she needs to know about this so they can be prepared." He clicked the phone on. "Hey, Mom."

twenty-five

M ick paced the kitchen floor, just as he had for the last thirty minutes. He had sat at the counter, numb from the revelations and the fact that Adam had chosen to go after her.

Asshole.

They had never had issues like this before, but then, they had never had another person in their relationship. Not for long periods at least.

He knew he had been the one to push this relationship, and it was mostly his fault, but they had proven it hadn't worked out. They weren't built for a permanent threesome.

"So, why is he over there and you're here by yourself?"

As if to answer the situation, his phone rang. Great. His mother. She would pick up that there was something wrong. He wasn't ready to talk about it. Still, if he didn't answer, there was a good chance she would continue to call, or worse, call Adam.

He clicked on his phone.

"Hey, Mom."

"Don't you hey Mom me."

"What?"

"I talked to Adam."

Well, shit.

"Yeah?"

"He explained the situation."

"How nice of him."

"Vincent McGrath, don't you use that tone with me. We will get to the state of the relationship in a moment, but you haven't called or texted. What would have happened if some tabloid had called me? I would have been blindsided."

"It just happened."

"Yeah, well, Adam had time to text and take my call."

Asshole.

"I wasn't ready to talk about it."

She sighed. "I understand it is still up in the air, but seriously, would you think this woman would do this for publicity?"

"She could have."

"But did she?"

Probably not. "She never told us about her past."

"Yes, but did you ask?"

"No, not really."

"I am disappointed in you. You know this young lady would not do this. Adam told me so."

"Mom."

"No. You will listen to me. You didn't want to ask her

because it would be something other than the fantasy you built in your mind. I love you, but you don't always look at the world and see the bad things."

Because it was close to the truth, he said nothing.

"And that poor girl, Serenity. She was in tears when I talked to her."

His stomach twisted. He had been extraordinarily cruel to her, and he wasn't a cruel person.

"She was crying?"

"You broke her heart."

He sighed. "She's not the only one hurting here."

"No, but you're the one doing most of the damage. Listen up. You are my baby boy and the light of my life. But from the way Adam talked about this woman, he's in love with her. I have a feeling you are as well. You screw this up, I will disown you and tell everyone you became a monk."

"What?"

"It's embarrassing that I have no grandchildren. You and Adam won't even talk of adopting. You both love this woman, so I have a real chance."

"I didn't know you would be so cool about this. It isn't normal."

"When have you ever been normal? How many sixteen year olds come out to their Army father to say they are bisexual? Not many, I'm sure. And, at the time, I'm pretty sure there wasn't that many fathers who would have accepted, especially a career Army guy. But he did...as did I. We both were happy when you and Adam finally settled down together, and while it is unorthodox, I am happy you found this Serenity."

"Mom." He didn't know what else to say. His parents were a little on the conservative side, but Mick had never questioned their support or loyalty. This, though, he hadn't been sure how his parents would take it.

"She sounds like a perfectly lovely woman, at least what little I talked to her. You love her. Adam loves her. And I'm fairly certain she is in love with both of you. Go fix things."

"I love you, Mom."

"I love you too. Now go."

She hung up the phone. He sighed. Now that his pain had subsided, he realized that it had been more to do with the fact that she hadn't told them everything. But his mother was right. He never asked Serenity. Not really. He hadn't pushed any more discussion about her past life. She hadn't been completely honest, but she hadn't ratted them out either.

His phone vibrated. He looked down.

Adam: *Get your damn ass over here and help me fix this.*

Dammit. He wasn't that good at groveling.

Mick sat there for a second or two trying to talk himself out of going over. It was safer to stay there, to just let the relationship dissolve. But, there was a tiny part of him that knew Adam might not side with him. After all the years of friendship and love, Mick might lose the one man he thought of as his soul mate.

But you don't have one.

That little voice in his head had been irritating him since

Adam had followed Serenity out the door. He hadn't thought further than getting Serenity in bed. He had wanted her on a level that he truly wasn't comfortable with. What had he thought would happen? That she would just be a fixture in their relationship and things would go on as they had before?

Damn, he was a dumbass. She was part and parcel of the whole now. Isn't that what he freaked out about last week? Bringing her into their bed, into their lives, had shifted everything. It was never going to be the same, but that wasn't always a bad thing. It would never be the same, but that also meant it was a new adventure. Truth was, he couldn't even fathom a relationship with Adam without Serenity.

He was absolutely going to have to grovel. With that thought in mind, he made his way over to her house. He heard Adam's voice, but he couldn't make out what he was saying. Every now and then, he heard a sniffle. Shit, his mother had been right. Serenity was crying.

Slipping off his shoes, he opened the front door without knocking. "He'll come around," Adam said.

"Maybe I don't want him to come around."

Adam's sigh was long and loud.

"He's a pain in the ass and he tends to act without thinking."

"That person isn't who I am now. Kayleigh died the day I changed my name, and I have never really looked back. Moving forward is the only way to survive."

"That's what they say about sharks."

"Great, now you think I'm like a shark. I really can't

believe I thought this would work. Two men is two too many."

"You don't think that."

"I do. I can't deal with the stress, and I will not be judged on things I did before I turned eighteen. Everyone was going to do that for the rest of my life. That's why I changed my name."

"So, why didn't you tell us?"

"Why didn't you ask?"

"That's a silly argument," Adam said. "Tell me."

Mick stepped into the room and saw her for the first time. Her face was splotchy from crying, her nose red, and she looked like crap.

And this had been his fault, dammit.

"Yeah, why don't you tell us?"

Her eyes narrowed. "I don't believe you deserve an explanation."

"Maybe not, but I think Adam does."

Her shoulders slumped and he regretted his comment. He knew she was hurting, and a lot of it was his fault.

"Fine. Tell me, what were you doing when you were sixteen? What embarrassing thing did you do? Or, let's dial back a year or two. Teen years suck. Think about if every transgression you had made was played out on the national stage."

That would not be good. He made a lot of mistakes in high school. Adam glanced at him and Mick saw the acknowledgement in his eyes.

"People don't know what you did then, except family. I

had cameras on me always and, yes, I pushed the limits. Most teens do. But yours wasn't recorded for everyone to see. Mine was and if I wanted people to take me seriously, I couldn't go by my stage name."

"That's not your real name?"

She shook her head. "Not sure. I think my mom changed it when she put me in show business, but I've never been able to find the documentation. So that's why I did it."

"Why didn't you tell us?" Adam asked quietly.

She studied Adam's face, then glanced at Mick.

"At first, it wasn't on purpose. It's ingrained in me. I said I was in show business and that usually works for people. Some will be intrigued, but the connections aren't there. It would take world class digging to figure out that I was Kayleigh Rose."

"But you continued on with the ruse. Why?" he asked. "Did you think that we would tell people?"

That thought had his heart hurting a little bit. He would never do anything to upset her or put her life in danger. It struck at his sense of protectiveness.

"It's because I didn't want you to know. I told you. I'm not Kayleigh Rose and haven't been for over a decade. I wanted you to take me for me."

"Do you think that we would do that?"

"I didn't know. When I'm sure I've moved on from the bullshit from my childhood, it pops up and smacks me. You both have become so important to me, I was worried about losing you. When you didn't ask, I felt it would just work out. I know it was stupid."

"Not stupid," Adam insisted. "Just, maybe shortsighted, like we were. I know I'm talking for both of us when we say that you don't have to tell us anything you don't want to. Just because this is out in the public now, that isn't important."

She looked at Mick. "Is that true?"

He didn't hesitate. "Yes. I don't want to lose you."

"But you would like to know." A statement and not a question.

He sat down on the bed next to her. "I want to know because it's a part of you. But we don't need an accounting of everything."

'That's not important right now. What's important is that we get ahead of this."

Her phone vibrated.

"Nicola," she said after picking it up.

She was quiet for a long period of time.

"I'm fine and no I'm not crying."

Quiet again.

"No, I don't need you to beat anyone up."

He shared a look with Adam.

"So, it was someone who saw me on the beach? How does something like that happen? I go to the beach all the time."

"Okay, okay."

The voice on the other end of the phone rose in volume.

"No, I haven't heard from her, but it won't be long, I'm sure. And, yes, I had a restraining order but didn't renew it."

Nicola talked for a long time, which had Serenity shaking her head and rolling her eyes.

"I told you before. I didn't want to do it because she would have my new name. You agreed."

She smiled.

"Yeah. Okay. And, yes, they're here."

She clicked on the phone speaker.

"So, I guess both of you are there," the crisp voice said on the other end of the phone.

"Yes," Adam said.

"Good. The best thing you can do is lay low. Are either of you going to have an issue at work?"

"No," Mick said. "We're independent and the company we contract with is owned by a close, personal friend. He already knows about the relationship."

"Good. Sometimes it's good to get out there with the info, but the truth is, Serenity is off the radar. If we can stop this information from leaking to the press, we can handle it easier. If not, a statement would be best. No personal appearances."

"Agreed," Serenity said.

"The best thing right now is that Hawaii has some strict laws when it comes to privately owned property. Anyone shows up and crosses that line, call the police."

"We can handle it," Mick said.

"No. Don't. Do not engage. Believe me, I've had to deal with this kind of stuff thanks to Jensen's past." There was a male voice, but he couldn't make out what the man was saying. "If you had kept it in your pants and hadn't become an addict, it wouldn't be a problem. Sorry about that. Jensen took umbrage to my comment."

"No problem," Serenity said with a smile.

"Remember, fake tabloid stories and rumors are best if you don't give them anything to print and threaten to sue."

"But our story is true," Adam said.

"Yes, but they don't have a right to it. None of you are public figures and have been living a quiet life. I'm going to talk to our lawyers about it, but I'm sure you can claim that any story would be detrimental to your ability to earn money, or something like that. I'll call you back after I talk to them. You call if that bitch calls, Serenity."

"Of course."

"Good. Our flight is about to take off and this is good timing. We had to be in Hawaii by Monday for a meeting, so we just moved it up a day. We should be there sometime in the middle of the night, but you know how to get hold of me on the plane.

"Yes."

"Now, go eat some chocolate."

Then she hung up.

"Wow. And that was your friend Nicola?" Mick asked.

She nodded. "Nicola McCann."

He searched his memory. The name was familiar, then he remembered the controversy. "The skater?"

She nodded. "She works for Jensen Wulf as his assistant."

"Wait, that was Jensen Wulf, billionaire, she was being rude to?"

She laughed. "She's always rude to him. I feel a little better that a reporter hadn't been the one to pick up on the story."

"We missed that part," Adam said.

"Oh, sorry. It must have been when we went to the beach a few weeks ago. Some tourist snapped a pic and didn't realize until later that it was me. They went to the *National Tattler* to sell the pic. They started to investigate from there."

"Do you think she can stop this?" Mick asked.

"Probably. She's kind of scary when she goes into this mode."

"I think we need to know more about your mother. She was the bitch Nicola was referring to, right?"

She nodded. "But like Nicola said, I need chocolate."

WITH HER BELLY FULL OF CHOCOLATE AND KONA Coffee, Serenity sighed and sipped her coffee. The guys had bought her a chair for the back lanai at their house.

She still cherished that thought. They hadn't even said a thing. They just walked out on the lanai. Her chair sat in between their own chairs. She was one of them.

"So, tell us about your mother," Mick said.

"I have. But, I think we need to be prepared that she knows, she will use it to get money for herself. She might be on TV a lot. And she will not hesitate to show up here and cause problems."

Adam blinked. "She would show up here?"

"Yep."

"Just like that. Knowing you're against it?"

"My mother has never thought about anyone but herself."

"Still?" Mick sounded incredulous.

She nodded then shrugged. "I would love to think she's changed, but I'm fairly certain she hasn't. See, she doesn't have to, so she won't. I think that's why she loves Hollywood. They don't force her to be anyone but the bitch she is. She fits in with a lot of the population. In the real world, she would be condemned for being a sucky mother. In Hollywood, it can be justified that she was trying to give me a future."

"But it wasn't your future, and it isn't what you want," Mick said.

"What did the folks say when you talked to Mom?" Adam asked.

"She kicked my ass, as you knew she would."

"And?"

She held her breath.

"She read me the riot act, then she said she wanted to meet Serenity."

"Just like that?" she asked.

"Yeah. My parents have always been a little unorthodox, especially for being military. They always accepted my relationship with Adam, and she's thrilled there's a woman in the mix."

"Why is that?"

"She wants grandchildren."

She choked on her coffee.

"Woah," he said, patting her on the back.

"Sorry." When she had control of herself again, she looked at them. "Babies?"

Mick and Adam shared one of those looks—the kind that she knew was a kind of secret communication. They turned back to her.

"We weren't going to broach the subject, but if we entered into a committed relationship, we wanted to build a life," Adam said.

"And that means babies?" she asked, trying to hold onto her emotions. She had often thought of having children, but she didn't know if it would ever happen.

Mick nodded. "It's not a deal breaker, but we both wanted to build a family. I mean, not right now. We would rather just be us for a while."

She thought about that. Just be us. That was a phrase she could get used to. She smiled and both men seemed to release a breath.

"I like the sound of that."

"Yeah?" Mick asked.

She nodded. "I just want to be us for a while too."

"So, this Nicola is going to fix everything?"

She nodded as her phone rang. Another California number.

"Hello."

When she heard the voice, her heart dropped to her stomach. It was the woman she had spent a decade avoiding, and the one who could completely ruin her happy life.

"Kayleigh, I finally found you."

"Hello, Mother."

twenty-six

Serenity felt as if she were living in a nightmare. First, the call from the tabloids. Then, almost losing Mick because of it. Now this.

Both men were staring at her as if they wanted to yank her phone out of her hands.

"I have been so distraught."

"Who's there?"

"What?"

"This performance has to be for someone. Who is it for?"

There was a beat of silence, confirming her suspicions.

"There is a reporter here, but—"

"Take me off speaker or I'll hang up."

"You should just hang up," Mick said. She glanced at the guys. Adam nodded. She knew that was what Nicola would suggest. No, Nicola would have gotten hold of the phone and blocked the number. But she had to let her mother know exactly where they stood.

"Okay," her mother said. Serenity heard the difference in the sound on the other end of the phone, telling her that her mother had turned the speaker off.

"I want to get one thing straight with you, *Mother*."

"I just wanted to talk to you. It's been over ten years since I've seen you and I've missed you every minute."

"You missed my money every minute."

"Kayleigh."

She cringed at the name. "My name is Serenity. Use it, or I hang up."

Her mother's sigh could be heard on the other end of the phone. "Okay, Serenity. I understand you're in a relationship with two men. You never could seem to keep yourself contained to one man."

"So, you call me after all these years just to insult me?"

"I didn't insult you."

"You called me a slut."

"I did not."

"Yeah, you did, but you did it in that way you have. It doesn't sound like an insult but it is."

"That was not my intention."

It was, but arguing about it would only keep her on the phone longer.

"Listen up, Mother. I do *not* want any contact with you whatsoever. I have no interest in doing any interviews. I won't ever act again, and even if I wanted to, you would have nothing to do with it."

"Kayleigh—"

"My name is Serenity," she said from behind clenched

teeth. "Now that everyone will know that, I won't hesitate to take out a restraining order...again. I will do it and make sure every reporter in Hollywood knows. Worse, I will make sure up and coming actresses know about you. That's what you're doing now, right? You're a talent scout?"

"I work for several studios." Her voice had turned mulish.

"How many of them would keep you on if they knew about our past? Do you still give kids valium, or have you moved on to OxyContin?"

"I have never done that."

"Really? Because I'm certain the rags don't care. Stay away from me, from my men, from everything to do with my life, or I will ruin yours. Do you understand?"

Another long moment of silence.

"Okay."

"Goodbye, Mother. And don't *ever* call me again."

Without waiting for an answer, she clicked her phone off. Then she blocked her mother's number.

She looked up at Mick and Adam.

"What?"

"Wow," Mick said with a smile as he unfolded himself from his chair. "You were badass."

She chuckled and he wrapped his arms around her and kissed the top of her head. Then he handed her off to Adam.

"Yeah, and I particularly liked when you said *my men*."

She smiled as he bent down to kiss her.

"It was definitely sexy."

She looked at them and recognized the looks. Before she

could respond, Mick was leading her back over to their house. And for now, that was all she needed. These men, this time, and their love.

JUST BEFORE DAWN, THE FLASH OF LIGHTS IN THE driveway caught Serenity's attention first.

She went to the window.

"Yay," she said, practically running to the door. Before Adam could stop her, she was out of the house and running toward their new arrivals.

"Finally," she said with a laugh.

Both he and Mick followed her out the door and watched as a statuesque woman unfolded herself from the town car before it had come to a complete stop. Adam could tell she was breathtaking, even with little light.

"Seri," she said, holding her arms open. Serenity walked right into them, and hugged the woman right back. Belatedly, they noticed a tall man walking towards them wearing a business suit and looking as if he had walked off a runway.

"Hullo, there. Sorry for the early intrusion, but Nicola wasn't about to wait to see Serenity. Jensen Wulf," he said with a smile. His accent was British and definitely upper crust.

"Oh, hello," Mick said a little breathlessly.

It was easy to understand. Even if Adam didn't know that Jensen Wulf was a billionaire or that he was part of a legendary family with ties to the Windsors, he was a striking figure. Okay, he was a fucking beautiful man. With the smile he offered, it was easy to see why he was often described as charismatic.

"Adam Fullerton, and this is Mick McGrath."

"Nice to meet you. Please tell me you have coffee, because my dragon of a PA refuses to let me have anything else."

"If you didn't crawl into a bottle every time you had a sip, you could drink anything you wanted. Good...I guess morning, yes?"

She still had one arm wrapped around Serenity as they walked up to the lanai side-by-side.

Jensen tossed a smile over his shoulder. "And, if I ever forget, you are here to remind me."

"Mick, Adam, this is Nicola McCann."

When she was close enough, Adam got a look at her eyes. Ice blue. He had seen pictures of her and video when she was competing, but nothing compared to the woman in person.

"Nice to meet both of you. And, as I'm trying not to be an ass like Jensen, who thinks the entire world works for him, I would dearly love some coffee."

MICK LOOKED THROUGH THE REFRIGERATOR AS HE planned breakfast. He assumed he would have to feed everyone after the night they had had.

It started with Jensen Wulf, who was completely different than he had expected. He had asked for a pillow, took off his shoes and jacket, and promptly fell asleep on

249

their couch. The noise didn't seem to bother him. Mick glanced over at the couch again and found the Englishman stretched out on the sofa, his feet dangling over the side.

"He sleeps anywhere," Nicola said from behind him. He turned to face Serenity's best friend.

"Yeah?"

She nodded. "I think it comes from his days as an addict. He would pass out and sleep wherever he landed. He's learned to shut noises out."

She turned back to the kitchen and he followed her. She'd taken off the killer heels, but still wore her short red skirt and blouse.

"So, you know him well?"

She nodded as she poured herself another cup of coffee. "Better than he knows himself. And I am going to get jitters from all this coffee, but I can't resist Kona coffee."

She doctored her coffee, then turned to face him, leaning back against the counter. The pose looked like she was relaxed, but he knew better. Both he and Adam were being assessed.

"Well, how do I hold up?" he asked.

Nicola smiled. "Quite well. She told me about your initial reaction to the rag story." He opened his mouth to defend himself, but she held up her hand. "No. It was understandable, in a way. And Serenity is always going to respond by walking away. Or will sometimes. She hasn't had a lot of people in her life do right by her, so it is her knee-jerk reaction."

He nodded.

"Now, I understand you are a world class cook."

"Is that what Serenity said?"

"Yes, but then she's in love, so you have to prove yourself to me."

Before he could respond, there was the sound of a car driving into the area. He looked out the kitchen window. A small rental parked in the street. A tall, slender man in his thirties crawled out. He reached back in to get a camera.

"Dammit," he muttered.

"What?" Nicola asked as she stepped up beside him.

"I think our reporter just showed up."

She didn't say anything, so he glanced at her.

"I know this bastard. Jerry Dawson. And I have his number."

She set the cup down and walked to the front door. He followed her and noticed that Jensen was sitting up and stretching.

"When's breakfast?" he asked.

"When I get done with this reporter," Nicola said as she slammed out the front door. Adam and Serenity were already hurrying from her house.

"Excuse me," Nicola said. "You are on private property."

The guy barely spared her a glance.

"Oh, this is going to be good," Jensen said. He glanced at the man. "Nicola loves to tear bad people apart."

The reporter tried to step around her, but she didn't allow for it. By now, Adam and Serenity had joined him. Serenity wrapped her arms around Mick and squeezed.

"I don't think you understood my comment," she said.

"I don't really give a damn. I'm here to talk to Kayleigh."

"There is no Kayleigh here. And besides, Jerry, I would start paying attention to the person who knows *your* name."

He stopped his forward progression.

"Listen, lady, I don't know who you are."

"Funny, but that makes me feel better. My name is Nicola McCann, and I'm the personal assistant for that man up there," she said pointing to Jensen. "Recognize him? Yes, that's Jensen Wulf."

The man opened his mouth to argue with her, no doubt, but she barreled ahead.

"I talked to your editor and to your paper's owner just this morning. You are not supposed to be here."

"I can sell to other papers." He offered her a smug smile. "Freedom of the press, lady."

Mick could tell from the way her back straightened, that she did not like that moniker.

"Oh, this bloke is digging his own grave," Jensen said beside him.

"Okay, so you're going to be an asshole. Let me explain to you something. See, I called HPD about you already."

He shook his head. "I haven't broken the law."

She pointed down to his feet. "You are standing on private property, but that's not what I'm talking about. When I got your name from your boss—yep, he handed you over—I spent a couple of hours researching your background. Do you know what I found?"

"No, what?"

"You're wanted in Illinois." The man's face turned white.

"Yep. I know about the four years of unpaid child support. I've alerted the authorities."

"That's not right."

"What? That I research a private citizen and turn their world upside down? It's all true. There's a warrant out for your arrest."

"She's not a private citizen."

"Yes. She is. But, you see, I only spent a couple of hours on you. I'm about to crawl up your ass—metaphorically speaking that is. By the time I am done with you, you're going to look at a colonoscopy as a playdate. I will find every little dirty deed you did. Wasn't your divorce because you liked to beat up your wife? Oh, and you had a taste for the hookers?"

His mouth opened and then snapped shut.

"You have about ten minutes before HPD shows up, so you should get out of here while you can, or you'll be snatched up as soon as they see you."

"I...goodbye."

The man turned around and practically ran to his car.

"Isn't she amazing?" Jensen said. The tone of his voice was filled with more than admiration.

"Yeah, she is," Adam said.

Nicola walked back. "That was easy."

"So, you let him off, just like that?" Adam asked.

Serenity laughed. "Not likely," she said. "Tell them. What did you do? I know you did something."

"HPD is supposed to gather him up at the airport."

"You are a mean woman, Nicola," Jensen said. "It's why you are the perfect PA for me."

She rolled her eyes. "Now, I believe breakfast was offered."

Mick smiled. "Anything for the woman who made that man almost wet himself."

She laughed as she walked toward their house. "I did do that, didn't I?"

AFTER AN AMAZING BREAKFAST, NICOLA AND Serenity had some time to themselves. She'd brought her best friend over to her house and they had looked over her new pics for the book. By the time they were done, Nicola looked ready to pass out.

"How many hours have you been up?"

"I caught a cat nap on the plane," she said, yawning. "Oh, excuse me. That was rude."

Serenity laughed. "I know you're tired when you start being proper."

She smiled as she settled down at Serenity's kitchen table. "I quite like your men."

Serenity returned the smile. "They make me happy."

"I can see that. I was ready to kidnap you if need be, but I don't think that will be necessary."

She shook her head. "Nope. We had a moment there, but...no. Everything is okay now."

"Just remember, those two are there for you. There will

be bumps. You just smack them and tell them to snap out of it. I have a feeling they will."

She nodded. "And you need someone now."

"Nope. Not for me. You know I don't work in that department since I lost Harry."

Serenity wanted to argue, but Nicola was tired, and that meant she could be mean. Plus, right now, she was just so happy being together with her best friend.

"You need sleep."

"That I do." She stood and pulled Serenity into a big hug. "I'm so happy for you."

"Thank you."

When she pulled back, she looked down at Serenity. Even with her shoes off, Nicola towered over her.

"I'll keep tabs on the other tabloids, but I haven't heard anything from any of the others."

"Good. Go get some rest."

She sighed. "Sounds brilliant."

Nicola wasn't English, but working with Jensen and his family had rubbed off on her.

"Just so you know," Nicola continued as she stepped out onto the lanai, "I'm going to book a spa day for us later next week."

Serenity smiled. "Like you said. Sounds brilliant."

―――――――

THE THREE OF THEM WAVED AT NICOLA AND

Jensen as they drove off. Adam really liked them, but he found Nicola a bit exhausting.

"Do they always have a driver?" Adam asked.

Serenity shook her head. "But when they arrive somewhere, it's to be expected. Ned goes with them everywhere. Along with Damon."

"Who is Damon?"

"Their pilot."

He stopped walking. "He has his own plane?"

"Of course he does," Mick said.

"It's Wulf Industries, but yes, they have their own plane. Makes more sense and thank goodness. It's the only way she could get here so fast."

They walked back into the house. "Coffee on the lanai?" Adam asked.

Mick and Serenity nodded. Five minutes later, they were sitting out back, Serenity between them. The day had started off hazy, but the temperature was rising and burning a lot of it off. He turned and glanced at Mick over Serenity's head. He nodded, telling him it was time they had *the* talk.

"Serenity," Adam started.

"Hmm?" she asked absentmindedly. She was leaning back in her chair and her eyes were closed.

"Mick and I wanted to have a talk with you."

She slowly opened her eyes. Wariness filled her expression. He gave Mick a dirty look.

"Don't look like that, please," Adam said.

"Like what?"

Her posture and tone said it all. She was rigid. Ready to

fight. He took her hand and gave it a squeeze. It took another second or two, but she relaxed.

"Sorry."

"No. We're sorry. We should have talked about this before, but everything happened so fast," Adam said.

"We wanted to make sure we were far enough away from the bed when we talked about it. We want you to know we're serious."

She sat back and looked from one to the other. "Serious about what?"

"You. And us," Adam said. "We want to make this official."

"In a ceremony?"

"That can come later," Mick said. "But, I guess we want you to know that we are cool with being your men. As in, a serious relationship."

"So, like we're going steady?"

Adam chuckled. "I guess you could call it that. We don't go for labels. We just wanted you to know that we see ourselves as a threesome now."

She didn't say anything for a long time. Then, her mouth curved and soon she was grinning. "I like the sound of that. But I have something to tell you."

"Is it worse than the tabloid crap?" Adam asked.

She shook her head. "That first time you guys had sex."

"With you?"

"No, in the house."

He looked at Mick, who was frowning at him. Then they both looked at her.

"Yeah?"

"I accidentally saw you."

There was a beat of silence. "Oh, so you're a voyeur?" Mick asked with a laugh.

"No," she said, her face turning pink. "It's just that I was taking pics and turned in your direction and accidentally saw you."

"And just kept looking?" Adam asked, laughing.

"No. Well, yes. I couldn't help it. You were both so...well, sexy. I couldn't help but look."

"We forgive you," Adam said.

She rolled her eyes. "I just wanted you to know. I've felt guilty all this time."

Adam shared a smile with Mick. He leaned down and kissed her, then Mick did the same.

"And don't worry," Mick said. "We'll talk about babies soon, but just so you know, Mom will be here next month. She'll be bugging you about it."

She covered her face with her hands. "Oh, God." She dropped her hands. "Maybe I need to do a shoot on Maui next month."

Adam laughed. "Good try, but now that you're with us, you have to deal with Estelle McGrath. But she's going to insist you call her mom."

Serenity smiled. "I really like the sound of that."

He picked her up off her chair and plopped her down on his lap. Mick moved over.

"What are you doing?" she asked.

"Just sitting here with my lovers, enjoying the fact we live in Hawaii."

"Sounds like a plan for today," Mick said.

"Yeah, it does," she said, as she settled back against his chest and Mick took his hand. As they enjoyed the sweet Hawaiian air and watched the beachgoers, Adam knew that now they had all found what they needed in each other. No one could ask for more than that.

epilogue

Five Years Later

Serenity tried to look down at her feet and sighed. She hadn't seen her toes in at least four weeks.

"Sit," Adam said as he walked into the kitchen.

Serenity rolled her eyes. The last nine months had been a lesson in patience. Both Adam and Mick had hovered over her like she was some fragile little thing. When she was diagnosed with gestational diabetes six weeks earlier, they had become impossible.

"I'm hungry."

He stepped closer, trailed his fingers down her arm. The calluses on his fingers never failed to send a frisson of heat through her.

"Come one. Sit down and I'll make you something."

Another sigh escaped before she could stop it. "I don't know what I want."

"Tell you what. Come on over here and sit down," he said, in that gentle voice she usually loved but now it irritated her. Still she said nothing because she knew he was just trying to help.

"What is going on here?" Mick said as he hurried in.

"Nothing. She's just a little out of sorts."

"I am *not* out of sorts. And I told you not to talk about me like I'm not here."

Both of them shared a look and she couldn't blame them. She was out of sorts. The trades had died earlier in the week, her lower back had been aching the last twelve hours, and she could only wear men's XL slippers because her feet were so swollen. She just couldn't get comfortable.

"How about some eggs?" Mick suggested.

"I think that might be too heavy."

"Fruit salad?" Adam asked.

She nodded. It didn't really sound good, but it was more appetizing than eggs.

As Adam prepared the fruit salad, Mick sat down beside her. She really was grateful for her men. They took good care of her and she took good care of them. Their relationship had only deepened over the last few years. She had never been so happy ever.

Just then, she felt a twinge in her lower back. This was worse than the others and she wasn't able to hide her reaction.

"What?" Mick asked.

"My back," she said, breathing through the pain.

He growled. "Come on. Let's sit on the couch."

Since that sounded lovely, she agreed. Taking his offered hand. The moment she stood, her head spun and she felt something pop before a gush of water.

"Oh, no," she said.

"What?" Adam said as he turned around. His eyes went comically wide before both of her men when into action. They quickly helped her clean herself, grabbed the go bag, and were on their way to Queen's Medical before she could even think of what needed to be done.

Serenity: *Well, my water just broke.*

Nic: *What? No. I am supposed to be there. That baby shouldn't go against my schedule.*

Serenity laughed. It was such a Nic comment.

"What?" Adam asked as he kept his eyes on the road.

"Nic is mad that our girl is coming early."

Mick smiled, but there was tension behind it.

"Don't worry. Everything is going to be okay."

"Are you trying to calm me down?" he asked.

"Yes. Because when we get to the hospital, I need both of you to be calm. You know I am going to freak out."

His shoulders settled and some of the tension drained from his expression. "I'll be calm once you are surrounded by a lot of beeping machines that tell us what is wrong."

She snorted. "There's nothing wrong. She's just impatient."

Thankfully, the traffic was light for mid afternoon and they made it to the hospital in record time.

"See, I told you," she said, as Mick rolled her into the hospital. Yes, they would not let her walk, so Adam was parking the car. By the time he joined them, they were already being led to her birthing room.

She smiled at her men as she settled into her bed. "See, this will all go smoothly."

Eight Hours Later

"I THOUGHT YOU SAID THAT WOULD GO smoothly," Adam said.

Okay, Serenity had been wrong. It had taken forever, and she wouldn't dilate, so after six hours, they had to do a c-section. It hadn't been her choice, but her blood pressure had gotten dangerously high. Thankfully, it went off without a hitch and they didn't have to put her to sleep for it so the guys could be in the room when Arabella was born.

She glanced up at the bandage on Adam's head. "I didn't know you would pass out."

Mick laughed so loud Arabella stirred in his arms.

"Shh," Serenity said with a smile. They have been back in her room for about thirty minutes and the guys kept taking turns holding their baby girl.

"Sorry, but that is never not going to be funny."

His eyes narrowed. "You didn't see it."

It was apparently a bit of blood that spurted. Big, bad Adam passed out.

Her phone buzzed and Adam handed it to her.

Nic: Pictures or it didn't happen.

Only her best friend would demand pictures of her child.

Serenity pointed her phone in the direction of Mick who was smiling down at Arabella.

Nic: Aww, that is one proud Papa. That girl is going to be spoiled. Thank them for keeping me updated. We will be there in about eight more hours after this refuel.

Serenity: I love you.

Nic: Love you, too. Now get some rest.

Serenity handed her phone to Mick who had already handed off Arabella to Adam who was settled in the chair. These men...she never thought she would find one man to love her, let alone two. But together, they made a family and she knew they would all love that little girl until the day they died.

With a sigh and a smile on her face, she settled back against her pillow and drifted off to sleep.

THANK YOU SO MUCH FOR READING HARMLESS Scandals! I hope you enjoyed it. If you did, please think about leaving a review on your favorite online store or review site.

If you want to find out what happens with Nicola, please check out Faith (formerly A Little Harmless Faith) releasing in October of 2024.

Be sure to check out the prologue of Faith.

faith

You met Nic and Jensen in Harmless Secrets, now check out
their book, *Faith*.

BUY THE BOOK

Four years ago

Jensen Wulf let himself into his New York brownstone and
sighed with relief. It had been a long three months since he'd

been here, in what he had termed as his sanctuary. He'd left on his own accord, ready to make a fresh start and walk away from the heroin haze he'd lived the last four years.

It smelled fresh. The vinegary scent of heroin no longer clung to the furniture. He assumed that his mother had made sure everything had been cleaned out before he returned. She was good like that. She kept their tidy even as everything else was falling apart. The floors had been redone, there was a new coat of paint...damn, he owed her.

He had disappointed her, more than a few times, but almost dying of an overdose was the worst. He would never forget the look of pain in her gaze. It was that look that had made him realize he wasn't just hurting himself.

There was mail stacked up on a credenza. His mother had taken care of the bills, he knew that. But, he was sure there was other correspondence for him. He picked up the envelopes and stepped into the living room.

He didn't see her at first. She was sitting in the chair to the right of the fireplace, her phone in her hand as she read something on the screen.

"I thought you would never make it in here."

American, but there was a slight accent to her voice that he couldn't place. She was dressed in a striking red blouse, a short black skirt, hose, and fuck me heels. Her hair was dark brown and long from what he could tell. She had it up in a ponytail. A black coat was draped over the arm of the chair.

"Excuse me."

She looked up at him. Ice blue eyes. Jesus, it didn't fit with the rest of the package.

"You spent a lot of time in the foyer."

He opened his mouth to explain why then he remembered it was his fucking house.

"Who the hell are you?"

She smiled, but there was little humor behind it.

"Nicola McCann."

The name was familiar but he was sure he had never met her.

"And you are sitting in my house for what reason?"

"Your mother hired me."

"For what?"

"I'm your sober companion. We're going to be best friends for the next three months."

acknowledgments

Once again, none of my books are ever released without the support of many people.

Big thanks to Noel Varner for kicking ass and doing great edits, once again.

No book ever sells without the help of a good cover. Scott Carpenter worked overtime and developed a whole new look for my Harmless books. I will be forever blessed that fate brought us together 13 years ago.

Thank you to Brandy Walker and Joy Harris for always lending me a sympathetic ear.

Shout out to the Addicts to always making me laugh and making our FB Aloha Friday Live events so much fun.

And, of course, there is my insane family. Thank you for putting up with the crazy author life.

about the author

From an early age, USA Today Best-selling author Melissa loved to read. When she discovered the romance genre, she started to listen to the voices in her head. After years of following her AF Major husband around, she is happy to be settled in Northern Virginia surrounded by horses, wineries, and many, many Wegmans.

Keep up with Mel, her releases, and her appearances by subscribing to her <u>NEWSLETTER</u>. If you want to keep up with cover reveals, new behind the scene info on her writing, and when new excerpts are posted, follow her MelissaSchroeder.net News News. Or you can do both! They are low traffic, so you will not get tons of emails.

Check out all her other books, family trees and other info at
<u>her website!</u>
<u>If you would want contact Mel, email her at: melissa@</u>
<u>melissaschroeder.net</u>

instagram.com/melschro

amazon.com/author/melissa_schroeder

facebook.com/MelissaSchroederfanpage

bookbub.com/authors/melissa-schroeder

goodreads.com/Melissa_Schroeder

tiktok.com/@melissawritesromance